Edgar Fawcett

Songs of Doubt and Dream

(Poems)

Edgar Fawcett

Songs of Doubt and Dream
(Poems)

ISBN/EAN: 9783744770316

Printed in Europe, USA, Canada, Australia, Japan

Cover: Foto ©Andreas Hilbeck / pixelio.de

More available books at **www.hansebooks.com**

Songs of Doubt and Dream

(POEMS)

BY

EDGAR FAWCETT

FUNK & WAGNALLS COMPANY

Toronto   1891   London

New York

CONTENTS.

Songs of Doubt and Dream.

THE BARTHOLDI STATUE.

(Unveiled on Bedloe's Island, October 28th, 1886.)

At last I loom in bronze o'er this wide bay,
And from the electric torch my starward wrist
Hath raised, for centuries I shall brave in calm
The lightning with the lightning.   I am bred
Of gods, for all high thoughts of men are gods,
And he, the poet of sculpture, from whose dreams
I rose like Troy from music, well doth know
His genius at my summons burst to power.
For he was earth, I light, he mortal, I
Divinity ; and man regenerate,
Shattering old thralls and gyves of shame and sin,
Desired me, and so needed I am come !
Or, truer yet, not verily I, but this
The symbol of my peace and sanctity ;
Since what in sooth I am is knit with laws
That whirl far planets round the fires of suns
Whose might ye gaze on but as darkling motes.

Nay, would I tell my lineage, for such task
The orchestral winds were tamer than a reed,
The blare of oceans weaker than a bird.
To learn from what dim ancestries I trace
Were to pierce time through æons back, and pause
Dazed at the lintels of eternity.

Here is my boon, ye people I would test.
Heed that ye use it well ; the choice is yours.
Much have ye done, yet much remains to do.
Ye fought with foes o'erseas until ye tore
This coign of continent from tyranny,
Standing thenceforth sublime in solitude
Among all nations.   Yet ye have not kept
Promise with your ideal, and threat to lapse
From the white summit of its dignities
More than ye grant this hour.   Democracy
Is louder on your lips than in your deeds.
The few grow sleek with gains that make their vaults
Harbors of futile treasure ; one throng sweats
For bread to breathe by ; one, still vaster, bows
In yokes of toil that drag it nigh the brute.
I speak not now of drones that drowse in sloth
And whose one proper wage is penury.
These are life's coarse guerillas that skulk sly

At the vague outposts of the gathering fray
And deem the rags their vice hath wrapt them in
Will pass for poverty's true uniform.
The rich among you cannot build their walls,
However spired or corniced, friezed or domed,
So dense that to the ears these pomps enclose
A cry of suppliant agony, demand,
Expostulation and untold rebuke
Will float not; cushions have no depth of down
And tapestries no plait of silk or wool
To dull the imperious passion of that cry.
Wan lips of labor freight the air with it
Till the new sunshine of each day has grown
A mockery of its torment, and the gloom
Of each recurrent night similitude
Of its dark sorrow. . . Whose the fault? Not mine,
For I am Liberty, and I, Liberty,
Am love, not hate—am fellowship, not pride—
Am duty and not indifference—help, not harm.

Look to it, O people, then, that this the flower
Of all republics bloom republican.
Let him that paves with bribes his path toward rule
Reach the shut doors of senates on maimed feet,
Burnt from the plowshares he himself hath lit.

Ordain that he who sells his vote for hire
Buys with such bargain crime's unflinching fee—
The chill strait cell, with loaf and jug to drown
Conscience in ghastly banquet. Crowd your schools
With learning and sweet discipline of chiefs
Versed in all wise experience, till their lore
Make Athens of your slums, and parents loth
To let their children drink at such pure streams,
Common as they are pure, be scathed with scorn.
Abase the vaunts of caste; your earls and dukes
Can win their earldoms and their dukedoms best
By that sole patent of nobility
A blameless manhood may confer on them,
Not by the coronets and strawberry-leaves
Dead kings have flung their bastards. Hold your arts
In reverence, and revering shield their rights,
Till he who tells with chisel, brush or plume
Your annals, may not starve at such high task ;
For poet, novelist, painter, sculptor, stands
Each as a firm caryatid that shall grace
The pediment of your unborn renown !

Last, look to it, ye that this mine image here
Should spur to chaste achievement, soilless end,
Look to it, I charge ye, lest corrosions dire,

And stealthy as they are dire, creep not to gnaw
With ruin's loitering fang your civic strength.
Recall, ye wrested from a thousand kings
Your commonweal, and with dry dust of thrones
Have blent the wash of sundering seas to make
Fit mortar for the granite of its towers.
Let them stay firm, ivied with histories
Of a most glorious past, that still shall keep
One deathless present.   Honor knows not time,
Being immortal, and man's love for man,

If once proved perfect in this faultful world,
Hath nor to-morrow nor to-day, but dwells
In zones of fame no dials calendar !

EVOLUTION.

Two flying forms, in pathless deeps of night,
  Watched the great spheres about them wheel and
    flame,
And many a planet, where it swept with might
  Round many a central sun, they named by name.

They spoke of races whom the gradual spell
  Of wisdom won had raised from crime and vice—
How hate and sin had made this world a hell,
  And love had made that world a paradise !

And while they singled, either near or far,
  Bright orb from orb in heaven's untold abyss,
At last one pointed to a certain star,
  And said, with dubious gesture, " What of this ? "

" Earth it is called," his musing mate replied,
  " By those dim swarms its continents beget.
'Tis a young star ; and they that there abide
  Shall not wear wings, like us, for centuries yet ! "

PEACE AND WAR.

A LARGE moon fired the drowsy east, and by the sad
      strange light she shed,
In meadowed sweep, in stony pass, you saw the land
      was dark with dead.

Aloof there loomed one solemn hill, and here a stately
      spirit stood—
An awful shape that stooped to wipe a massive sword
      that dript with blood.

So stooping, then, the spirit heard a sound of murmur-
      ing, mild and low:
"At last thy red reign hath an end; wipe thou thy
      bloody blade and go!"

And now the spirit rose to turn his cold contemptuous
      eyes on one
With whose white brow it was as when the morning
      sea first feels the sun.

And front to front as gods they stand, both silent fo
    a fleeting while,
War with his harsh hard reckless face, and peace witl
    her benignant smile.

War curls his dark lip in a sneer, sheathes his grea
    sword, and answers then :
" I go, yet who shall say I go, while hate is hate, .
    while men are men ? "

A NINETEENTH CENTURY KING.

(*He Muses.*)

IF I believed the souls august
Of ancestors that long are dust
Beheld me at this hour, 'twould wake
Shame in my own soul, keen of ache !
For their dim ghosts would seem to chide
From shadowy vantages of pride,
Their hollow eyes would seem to hold
Remonstrance and rebuke untold,
Their spectral lips would seem to rain
On my degeneracy disdain.
Yet well I know their sculptured tombs
Enwrap them with eternal glooms,
And if at all their force and fire
In spheres remote achieve, aspire,
No heed nor knowledge irks them there
Of this poor crown I tamely wear—
This crown they caught and clutched for years
Through history's tides of blood and tears.
Even now, perchance (who dares be sure ?)
In stars unguessed their days endure,

With memories of their earthly rank
Faded to one forgetful blank,
And all their splendors of renown
Lost in the lots of clod and clown.   .   .
Nay, ghosts I fear not; many a fear
More fleshly steals to haunt me here.
For how am I, thus girt by thrall
Of quickening freedom, king at all?
My parliaments, whose rafters ring
With statesmen's edicts, ask no king.
My people, in whom obeisance lay
Invulnerable but yesterday,
Are now a throng of myriad throats
Voicing their individual votes,
Dictating laws, ordaining plans—
In all save name republicans.
And they whom my forefathers held
Stanchest auxiliaries of eld,
My nobles, born custodians, each,
Of every verge my sway doth reach,
Are stripped of all their state once meant,
Save empty and idle precedent.
No more about the throne's proud piers
They group its guardian halberdiers,
With loyalty in their least breath

And duty another word for death.
Their sires' tough mail-shirts they forsake
For broadcloth garb of modish make ;
In them the rough allegiant oath
Is dainty deference touched with sloth ;
The swords bold warriors joyed to hurl
Are canes that smooth hands lightly twirl ;
The intrepid charger, wild of breed,
Has grown the equestrian's neat-groomed steed ;
The bluff retainers, hot for fray,
As liveried lacqueys cringe to-day.

What wonder I should deem it strange
To rule a realm so swept by change,
Where only in legend now may live
The sovereign's lost prerogative ?
What wonder I should long to flee
This hollow and senseless pageantry,
That sets me in mimic schoolboy dread
As its imperial figure-head—
Between a thousand schemes, plots, lies,
Flaunted the incarnate compromise !
No part bear I in civic strife
That pricks conservatisms to life
And makes the wound thus dealt them fill

With liberty's awakening thrill.
Aloof I dwell, by power disowned,
A mere tradition crowned and throned !
I sometimes dream that I can trace
Insidious mockery in the face
Of him who leans most low to kiss
My hand, with courtliest emphasis.
I sometimes fancy I almost feel
Attendants at my side conceal
Thoughts they would tremble to declare,
Yet whose dumb sarcasms freight the air !
At balls of pomp, while flattery floats
Among my beams her myriad motes,
While sycophancy's unctuous phrase
Forgets the false heart it betrays,
While caste from reverent censer swings
The dizzying vapors dear to kings,
While fashion, where my foot hath trod,
Spaniels for one consentient nod—
Oh, then I hear the night-winds wake
Through many a distant dell and brake,
Where moon may brood or planet shine
On lands that are yet are not mine !
Then yearn I for the bounteous balms
Of nature's clamorings or her calms—

The unfevered life, the fretless hope,
The horizon of divulgent scope,
The statecraft of the stealthy seeds,
The wide democracies of weeds,
The birds' patrician claims of class,
The prosperous commonwealths of grass,
The ministries of heat or cold,
The sun's exchequer of lavish gold,
The blithe republics of the bees,
The butterflies' buoyant anarchies,
The oratory of air and cloud,
With leaves for listeners, low or loud,
The church of meadow and copse and hill,
The ritual of the brawling rill !

Two rival natures in my breast
Contend with terrible unrest.
One through dead lines of kings I draw,
And one through life, love, knowledge, law.
One breathes of feudalism that made
My sires the autocrats they staid ;
One hates the barriers reared to ban
His individual rights from man.
One, howso'er its chill duress
Enchain me, I know for selfishness ;

One stirs me to the inmost soul
As conscience, wisdom, self-control.
One means the past, whose purlieus throng
With every emissary of wrong ;
One means to-day, whose daring ken
Bears priceless promises to men !   .   .   .
Yet strong though each persuasion speak,
The instinctive bonds of birth grow weak;
Progress, a spectre keen of eye,

Stands at my gate, like Mordecai ;
Through many an empty palace-hall
Sad voices of the unsheltered call ;
I count my glittering gems, and feel
What human miseries they could heal ;
I read the tales deft scribes have wrought
Of how my great forefathers fought,
And lo ! their glory of field and flood
Hideous with war's reproachful blood !
I scan the Bible in which their pride
Found slavery's outrage justified—
The murder of little children not
Diabolic—treachery's vilest plot
Against a foe shorn clean of sin—
And from such chronicles I win
Disgust in place of reverence, hate

To accuse, not heart to venerate !
Search as I will through ancient things,
Divinity deserts all kings ;
Delve as I will through things that are,
Divinity flies yet more far ;
Dream as I dare of things unborn,
Divinity ossifies to scorn !
For centuries while their rulers built
Empire on rapine, greed and guilt,
The people had slept in dreamless trance,
Lulled by their opiate, ignorance.
But slowly at last they woke from sleep ;
Their great sigh surged from deep to deep ;
The opening of their drowsy eyes
Burned like dawn's flame in cloud-hung skies ;
At every stir their roused limbs gave,
Some tyranny tottered to a grave ;
And when, erewhile, erect they rose,
The world was rent with earthquake throes.

You people, ah, what resorts have we,
Kings, councillors, when such as ye
Break bonds whose links we forged and set,
To beard us with our unpaid debt !
A little while demur we may,

With this expedient, that delay;
A little while you mark what shade
The dial of destiny has made.
We smile, propitiate, condone,
We parley and quibble and postpone.
But in the end no guile will serve—
You still demand, nor deign to swerve!
O people, I know you where you press
Against my throne's gilt rottenness;
I know your impetus was fed
By despotisms of epochs dead;
I know you dowered with might that comes
From ancestries of martyrdoms.
Inch by stern inch our treasured shrine
Of sovereignty you undermine;
You brook no dexterous feints and tricks,
No parry-and-thrust of politics.
On your rebellions, which are fate's,
Legality idly legislates.
As well dig dungeons to ensnare
The lightning's blade, the thunder's blare;
As well with scourges lash the main
Or discipline the hurricane;
As well rear scaffolds cubits high
To strangle truth's white throat thereby,

Or steal from Time the scythe he bears
To assassinate him unawares—
As well all this, O people in whom
Revolt is degradation's tomb,
As curb you, crush you, towering here,
The immitigable mutineer !

THE OTHER SIDE OF THE MOON.

SHE turns her great grave eyes toward mine, while I
     stroke her soft hair's gold ;
We watch the moon through the window shine ; she is
     only eight years old.
"Is it true," she asks, with guileless mien, and with
     voice in tender tune,
" That nobody ever yet has seen the other side of the
     moon ? "

I smile at her question, answering "yes ;" and then, by
     a strange thought stirred,
I murmur, half in forgetfulness that she listens to every
     word :
" There are treasures on earth so rich and fair that they
     cannot stay with us here,
And the other side of the moon is where they go when
     they disappear !

" There are hopes that the spirit hardly names, and
     songs that it mutely sings,
There are good resolves and exalted aims, there are
     longings for nobler things ;

There are sounds and visions that haunt our lot, ere
    they vanish, or seem to die,
And the other side of the moon (why not ?) is the far
    bourne where they fly !

" We can fancy that realm were passing sweet and of
    strangely precious worth,
If its distant reaches enshrined complete the incom-
    pleteness of earth !
Nay, if there we found, like a living dream, what here
    we but mourn and miss,
Oh, the other side of the moon would beam with a glory
    unknown in this ! "

"Are you talking of heaven?" she whispers now,
    while she nestles against my knees,
And I say, as I kiss her white wide brow, " You may
    call it so, if you please ;
For if any such wondrous land may be, and we journey
    there, late or soon,
Then from heaven, I am sure, we shall gaze and
    see . . the other side of the moon ! "

MARRIED BOHEMIANS.

Oh, Meta, quit the prosy task that frets
　　With seams and hems monotonous of hue,
Your two dear eyes, those timorous violets
　　That never yet have lost their morning-dew.
For now the city spires are tolling nine,
　　And low the elastic night-wind breathes of June,
And lengths of dusky avenues weirdly shine
　　In murmurous life below the summer moon.

Take down that blossoming bonnet I adore
　　And let us ramble among the sombre streets ;
This embryo manuscript that floods my floor
　　May dry at leisure its chaotic sheets.
I leave my heroine hard-beset by fate　.　.　.
　　What merciless torturers we scribblers are !
But then I have promised her to sit up late
　　And end her miseries with my last cigar.

How gladdening, now the open air is gained,
　　To feel in mine your soft arm rest and cling !
Thank Heaven its lovely roundness has not waned
　　Since first your white hand wore my wedding-ring !
For though precarious days have hurt me sore
　　Through fears for that sweet wife I would protect
The stealthy wolf that prowls from door to door
　　Still treats our own with amiable neglect.

How many a favored lord or lover true
  Walks with the woman of his choice, at ease
Below this tender sky's more liberal blue,
  On spacious lawns, to-night, by whispering seas !
For them the illumined sward that sinks or swells,
  The breeze that wanders over meadowy miles ;
For us the sleepy treble of street-car bells,
  And street-lamps glaring in long fiery files.

And yet the ardor of something to attain
  Far deeplier than attainment may delight;
With all our stately castles off in Spain,
  We still possess them by signorial right.
We dine each evening on no sumptuous fare,
  Yet while the imposing future fails to frown,
Across indifferent claret both declare
  That my new tragedy will storm the town.

Ah, lovelier to my soul than speech may name
  Is the fond thought that if my stars allow,
We two shall reach the flowery paths of fame
  Joined arm-in-arm together, just as now !
But if the austere old gate shall never let
  Our envious feet those welcome gardens win,
Secure from discontentment we shall yet
  Have all Bohemia to be happy in !

A RETROSPECT.

WANDERING where mortals have no power to gauge
  The enormity of night that space outrolls,
Floated or paused, in shadowy pilgrimage,
  Two disembodied souls.

One towered a shape with dark wild-trailing shroud,
  With face by sorrow and anger seamed and drawn ;
One loomed a holy glory, as when some cloud
  Swims deep in baths of dawn.

World after world they gazed on, till beguiled
  They flew toward earth, and hovering where she
    swept,
One with a saturnine dejection smiled,
  And one with slow tears wept.

" On that star," said the spirit of sombre mien,
  " As Dante I passed through pain's most blinding
    heats " . . .
" On that star," said the spirit of look serene,
  " I suffered, and was Keats !"

NEBUCHADNEZZAR'S WIFE.

OVER Babylon's grandeurs one grayness of ominous
  mist had outrolled;
To their altars the priesthood had hurried, with
  visages white to behold;
Now the mirth of the shawms and the sackbuts by
  night or by day did not ring,
And the people were huddling in terror, for the curse
  had come down on the King.

They were wailing for Nebuchadnezzar, and none who
  had heard them could tell
If to Asshur in anguish more noisy they prayed than
  to Nebo or Bel;
For the great sacred river was glooming, as though
  some fell deed had been done
Between Supulat, god of Euphrates, and Shamas, god
  of the sun.

And in street, garden, square, or in temples, with their
  ziggurats' towering pride,
There was lamentation more dreary than if Ishtar the
  deathless had died.

They had heard how the Jewish Jehovah his burden
    of penance could bring,
But they sought the old gods of their people, for the
    curse had come down on their King.

Through the city one deep desolation had banished by
    spells of affright
The turmoil of traffic at noonday or the toss of the
    torches at night.
Over Nebuchadnezzar's vast army one sorrowing
    stupor would drowse,
Alike on the helmeted spearmen and the archers with
    filleted brows.

In the market-place gathered no buyers where the
    fruit-sellers' booths overran
With grapes from Kasvin and with quinces from the
    orchards of Ispahan.
All day on their slabs in the sunshine the eels from
    Aleppo would bake
Unbought near the barbel from Tigris and the black-
    fish from Antioch Lake.

No Assyrian maiden looked longing at the riches that
    merchants unfold ;
At the agates and sards from Choaspes in their fili-
    greed Indian gold ;

At the onyxes from Susiana, at the Bactrian jewel or
    jar;
At the pearl-crusted broideries from Persia, or the
    muslins from Malabar.

With safety the ibex would wander on slopes where
    the tamarisk dwells;
With safety at pools in the meadows would pause the
    pale-spotted gazelles.
Where the eyes of the lions flamed yellow, their sleek
    bodies trembling to spring,
No more betwixt reeds of the rivers the arrows from
    chariots would sing.

No more to far countries Caucasian the venturing
    huntsmen would ride
Where the aurochs in aisles of the forest black-maned
    and majestic abide;
No more on big beasts lying slaughtered, when dumb
    was the chase with its din,
Would they pour the red sacred libations in homage
    to Nergal or Nin.

But I, in my bonds of bereavement, through reveries
    no cheer could console,
I would pace my long tapestried chambers, on my
    couches of ivory would loll;

And of throngs that lamented their monarch, unto
    none came affliction more keen
Than to me, his moon-browed Amyitis, his beloved
    Babylonian queen.

He had wooed me with ardors of passion ; he had won
    me to share his great throne ;
For I was imperial, a princess, with lineage as proud
    as his own.
In the halls of my fathers he found me, at the first
    flush of girlhood's young dream,
Where the mountains of Media are mighty and the
    domes of Ecbàtana beam.

He had wed me and girt me with worship ; he had
    built me, to ban my least cares,
Hanging gardens where fountains of porphyry played
    splendid from flowery parterres ;
He had clad me in tissues like cobwebs, where
    diamonds like dew shed their sheens,
And the robes of the slave-girls that fanned me were
    fit for the ransoms of queens.

Ah, many an evening together, when sunset its breezes
    would waft,
In the dusk of my silken pavilions the wines of
    Armenia we quaffed.

Flung below me, his dark brawny beauty from the
tiger-skins gleamed to my gaze,
And like wrath in the green eyes of dragons his arm-
lets of emerald would blaze.

But 'twas love, only love, that illumined his looks when
they dwelt upon mine,
As I called him my conqueror, my hero, my warrior,
my chieftain divine.
And we lifted our rose-wreathen goblets, we fed upon
love's richest fruits,
While from clustered acacias came floating the music
of Palmyrene lutes.

At a word he would gladly have given me the choicest
of war-plunders rare,
Between walls of the seven-colored temples piled gorgeous in layer upon layer ;
Yea, his mandate had molten to please me—so dear
was my whim's lightest nod—
The two holy serpents of silver that coiled below Bel-
tis, their god !

But the crafty Judæans he had vanquished wrought
slow on the moods of his mind,
Till I hated the wizardries guileful that round him like
skeins they entwined ;

For at last he would come to me sombre where jovial
    erewhile he had come,
And the beam in his dark eye was clouded, the laugh
    on his bearded lips dumb.

Then he spoke of a dream that had irked him, filled
    full of inscrutable threat,
But I bade him disdain and forget it, as kings may
    disdain and forget ;
Yet alike my entreaties or counsels were emptier than
    air to his ears,
And he passed from my portals desponding, though I
    strove to detain him with tears.

Through the morrows that brought him not near me,
    I languished with longing supreme,
And I learned how an Israelite prophet had risen to
    interpret his dream ;
How monitions that teemed with disaster were spoke,
    and had stricken him as true,
By the man that was now Belteshazzar, but once had
    been Daniel, the Jew.

And no more to my bowers would he wander, and
    ever my torment was worse,
Till at last came the message of misery, the tidings
    that told of his curse.

And hearkening I trembled for horror when they whispered with gasps of their King
That he prowled the great park of his palace, a prone
graminivorous thing !   .   .

Then the frenzy of awe seized our city, as through it
this grim story shot,
And in tumult, alarm, consternation, Amyitis, the
Queen, was forgot.
But I spake to my tiremaids with calmness ; I lulled
their fierce fears into rest,
Though my pulses like snared birds were fluttering,
the heart was on fire in my breast.

So erelong to the chief of the eunuchs I bade that a
message be sent :
Untarrying he came where I waited, and low in obeisance he bent.
And I said to him, " Aspenaz, hearken, as thou hast
been faithful and true,
For strange is the task that in secret thy queen shall
command thee to do."

Then I told my desire, and he started, and prostrate
he fell in dismay,
And " O Queen !" he responded, " thy servant but
lives thy behests to obey.

"Still, pause . . for too rashly thou temptest the
    gods in omnipotence dread——"
But I towered o'er him, quivering with anger, and
    answered him, " Slave, I have said !" . .

How loitered those leaden-shod moments till midnight
    made good her mute reign—
Till I passed the unchallenging swordsmen that guard
    my seraglio's domain—
Till I reached the great hall of the palace, with lines
    of dim lamps by the score
Clinging chained to its big cedarn rafters and starring
    its long marble floor !

And here through the vague light to meet me came
    Aspenaz, potent with aid ;
Though rebellious at first from sheer pity, at last he
    had humbly obeyed ;
And together in silence we glided past walls painted
    fair, near and far,
With the deeds of divine Hasiadra and of bull-slaying
    Idzubar.

But by narrower corridors wending, we gained the
    immense palace-park,
And I felt the fresh breeze on my forehead rush fleet
    from the distances dark.

Just beyond were the dense trees, and o'er them such
    night as no meanest cloud mars,
For all of Chaldea to be wise by, spread legions of
    sibylline stars.

Then, terrace by terrace descending, we stood where
    the grass dripped with dew. . .
" Now," I whispered to Aspenaz, "leave me." . .
    He shuddered, and softly withdrew . .
Like a vanishing phantom I saw him retire and be
    lost up the slope . .
He had left me alone with my longing, my pain, my
    despair and my hope !

Then I dropped on my knees in the darkness and
    stretched forth my arms to its air,
As though I could clasp and possess it because my
    beloved one was there ;
And I cried , " O my King, I await thee, whate'er be
    thy doom or thy dole !
Let the gods work their worst on thy body ; not that
    do I seek, but thy soul !

" Come hating me—fear shall not fright me, nor pride
    my quick pardon efface !
Come . mad—I will soothe thee to mildness ; come
    brute-like—my arms will embrace !

Come deformed—I shall know thee and love thee!
Come hideous—thou shalt not repel!
Thou art heaven to me always, though branded with
scars from the forges of hell!"

. . . Was it wind in the trees? Was it movement
of deer through the foliage dank?
I knew not, but listening and yearning, low down in
the darkness I sank.
Still the sound, stealing nearer and nearer—still the
sound, creeping close—but no sight,
Save the lawns that flowed black all about me, and the
stars overhead that burned white.

Did I dream? Was the darkness dividing? Had he
heeded the prayer I had prayed?
Then a voice. . . It was his, yet so mournful!
. . "*Amyitis, art thou not afraid?*" . .
"No! no! no!" I flashed forth . . and so speak-
ing, I gazed where he grovelled supine,
One rank detestation and horror, fit consort for earth-
searching swine!

But I shrank not an instant before him; unreluctant I
leaned and embraced;
Had I clung to him glorious and stately, to spurn him
now, spoiled and defaced?

And I cried, "Whatsoe'er thine abasement, low down
    to it, lord, let me bow !
Though the barrier between us be loathsome, still,
    love, I am I, thou art thou !"

.   .   .   .

Night by night we met thus till the bondage that fet-
    tered and foiled him had ceased,
Till he rose once more Nebuchadnezzar, he rose dis-
    enthralled and released.   .   .
All the people have hailed him with welcomes till their
    gladness the land hath o'erflowed,
But on me, Amyitis, adored one, his dearest of smiles
    are bestowed !

AT A WINDOW.

Dawn drowns the stars while still the city sleeps;
O'er swarms of dusky roofs one pallor creeps.
My little chamber-window towers so high
That even so shame-beset a thing as I
May get some sort of kinship with this chastity of sky.

Once I was clean of spirit as are they,
Maidens, that dream pure dreams, not far away—
Maidens, with marriage-vows from lovers true,
With love to shield, with no rash deed to rue,
With all life budding like a rose and sparkling like its
    dew.

How shrill the heavy carts go clattering past—
Clattering while shattering this dead calm at last !
And hark ! off yonder, where the dulled lamp flares,
A woman blends with the wild oath she swears
Laughter that, ere you lose it, seems half sin's voice,
    half despair's.

A few short years, and I shall be like her,
Unless death strike me first, and so deter
The black degeneration that must wring

From my lips, too, below its goad and sting,
Curses and blasphemies like those I heard that harlot
fling.

There is a door-yard where this morn of May
Broods on the lilacs with their flowers in spray;
There is a threshold I no more shall cross,
Dim with the desolation of my loss—
However lightly o'er its verge the vines may flash and
toss.

And I am here—wife, mother, daughter, I
That was all three, slew each, yet fail to die !—
Whose madness was a challenge hurled at fate,
Who hear my own stabbed conscience moan "too late,"
Who, though I had won home's heaven of love, dared
the world's hell of hate !

I sometimes dream that I can look on those
Deserted for the infamy I chose . .
That I can see *him* sitting with bowed head
Among the children I have forfeited,
And by his bloodless cheek discern how his torn heart
has bled !

Perchance a child may come to clasp his knee
And question him in wistful words of me,

And answering, he may struggle to conceal
The outrage and revolt he still may feel,
Yet mould to a lie of mercy all his language might
　　reveal.

I value not that peace whose calms begin
When pity-of-self plays juggler with our sin ;
I am not one to stammer ere she name
The length and breadth and blackness of her blame ;
My shame stares naked at me now, nor less nor more
　　than shame.

I might in time have paused ; the abyss I grazed
Was not so bowered in bloom but had I gazed
Closelier I could have seen, beyond its rim,
That dizzying sweep to degradation's dim
Lair of the imperilled life, the broken and bleeding
　　limb.

So, then, the bound being taken, I arose
Maimed, staggering.   He that sprang with me ?   God
　　knows
Whither his coward feet unharmed had fled . .
I had fallen, and fame, repute towered lost o'er-
　　head . .
I had fallen ; abased and thick with thorns the path I
　　now must tread !

Wounded, I have trod it. Lower, year by year,
It slopes, and ever loudlier I can hear
Voices of memories, loves, remorses, roll
And echo and interblend amid my soul,
Reeling toward darkness where even death might
  shudder while it stole.

Nay, death's corruptions are to stains like these
Purity ! . . and alas, by slow degrees
I sink ! for it was only of late I let
Wine work its opiate freaks with my regret,
But nightly I now desire, need, crave the trance its
  fumes beget !

How sluggishly that tired boy slumbers there,
With brow so white beneath his gold of hair !
I wonder if awakening he at least
Will know me? or had recollection ceased
Long ere we met last night, he giddy and fevered from
  his feast ?

At any moment round him he may peer,
While mists of stupor from his vision clear ;
And then, remembering, he may strive to show
A vestige of the kindly and tender glow
His frank young eyes turned full on mine a few brief
  hours ago.

And then . . the night's dead spell, the day's live
    beam
Off my true self will mercilessly seem
To strip its cheat and sorcery, till I stand
Before him, scathed and blemished with that
    brand
Of crime whereby his worthier self was ravaged and
    unmanned.

But he alertly as would some breeze that flings
A loose leaf from the stalk whereto it clings,
Will cast all remnant of disgrace aside—
So soon exonerated, justified,
That even the mother who bore him might perchance
    forget to chide.

" Men will be men, and youth is fire, not snow ;
Wild oats were meant for such as he to sow
In merrymaker's folly or drift of whim . .
He's plenty of time to grow sedate and grim " . .
How surely all the old commonplaces hedge and shel-
    ter *him !*

But ah, we women ! if we fall, we fall !
Our cup is brimmed, and we must drink its gall
Down to the dregs, whatever bane they be !

No chance of pity, of hope, for such as we ! . .
How sternly all the old commonplaces crush and shat-
ter *me !*

I, woman, if I sin, must face the doom
Of one drear future's ignominy and gloom ;
Pardon, for me, grows unrelenting scorn ;
My mirth or tears, though I may laugh or mourn,
Are loathsome as the vesture that a leper's body has
borne.

Repentance has for me no boon of peace,
No rehabilitation, no release ;
Protest, prayer, supplication—all invite
A losing battle ; I feel, howe'er I fight,
The dagger of odium pierce me and the scourge of
censure smite.

Meek charity, ever rich in healing balms,
Has naught for me save pauperdom's cold alms ;
The liquid eyes of love itself have grown
A gorgon's glare that changes me to stone . .
What wonder I still sin on, being so forsaken, so alone !

For one at least may get the chance to win
A kind of ghastly comfort out of sin ;
A comradeship is here, however vile,

A human interchange of speech and smile,
A power by some faint spark of cheer guilt's night-
    mares to beguile.   .

And he erelong will rise and go his way,
Forgetting me, I doubt not, in a day ;
On him indulgence and exemption wait ;
His fault as mine was every whit as great ;
But ah, he is man, and therefore could be safely profli-
    gate.

What mockery is at root of laws that rust
In creeds of preëlection so unjust ?
If sin be sin, what preference bids it scan
With lowering looks of punishment and ban
The woman it enslaves and soils, yet pause to absolve
    the man ?

Hath he not made his path of daily use
Teem with extenuation and excuse ?
Customs and codes that for the man express
Freedom, are wrought the woman to oppress ;
Woman must bend herself to these, or break below
    their stress !

I, shall I stumble on with burdening gyves ?   .   .
The city wakes, yet from its myriad lives

Which of them all than mine draws wearier breath ?
Ah, still, at least, whate'er the proud world saith,
Even one debased as I may reach the dignity of death!

I think the meanest life can somehow save
A trace of hidden grandeur for its grave—
Something that speaks to impious or devout
Through just this going away and passing out
Into the mystery and the dark, the silence and the
    doubt.

I, if I went like that, might thrill to see
Eternity between my shame and me !—
Might leave the accursed part I well may spare,
Here like a garment flung for beasts to tear,
While she who had worn it rushed to find some refuge
    .   .   God knows where !

To close the eyes—to clench the teeth—to steel
The nerves, no matter how your brain may reel
Or the heart thunder in your breast and ears !
Then, leap ! . . and onward, then, through all
    time's years,
Oblivion follows, voiceless victor of disdain's worst
    jeers !

                    (*She leaps into the street below.*)

BIRD-LANGUAGE.

HARK, love, while through this wood we walk,
  Beneath melodious trees,
How wrens with redbreasts ever talk
  What tuneful words they please.

Lured by their feathered clans and sects,
  The listener lightly notes
Those airy and dulcet dialects
  That bubble from birds' throats.

Ah, joy, could we once clearly greet
  The meanings gay that throng
Their silvery idioms and their sweet
  Provincialisms of song!

No graybeard linguist, love, could vie
  With our large learning, then!
You'd speak to me in Redbreast; I
  Would answer you in Wren!

A CITY ECLOGUE.

At times it is my choice to go
Where spread the city's regions rude,
Where poverty clasps hands with woe
And all is dingy desuetude.
Nor do I nurse this nomad mood
When night hangs dark o'er lairs forlorn,
But when day's full divulging glow
Smiles ignorance and sin to scorn.
I seem at hours like these to know
The miseries and misdeeds of man
In piteous nudity that means
How slight a variance intervenes
To part myself from those I ban
As bordering on barbarian.

I mark a hundred coarser throes
Of mind and heart than one may meet
Where sweeps the daintier-tended street
Below patrician porticoes.
Here greed forgets its fang to hide ;
Black envy scowls with hardier hate ;

Here from the inclement eyes of pride
A fiercer flame will scintillate.
In raw contempt of codes that chide,
The quick curse leaves the reckless lip;
More frequent fume the froths of strife;
More blunt the jeers, more bold the lies,
As though from loins and limbs of life
Rough candor strove with zeal to strip
Its best expedients of disguise.

Yet even amid such movements made
By poverty's drear masquerade,
Continually I discern
Similitudes at every turn
Between the souls with want o'er-weighed
And those whom kindlier fate has lent
Prosperity's enfranchisement. . .
This trundling dame, with ragged gown,
Who prowls in gutters to secure
Stray refuse purer than the impure
Flotsam and jetsam of the town,—
What feint of fancy bids me find
The imperfect portraiture in her
Of caste's contented dowager?
Environment, with sombre thrall,

Has bid her forage thus for bread ;
One stroke of change, and lo, she had led
Serene gentility in all
The proud pomp of its choicest ball,
Brocaded and bediamonded ! . .
Or yet the inactive tramp who lolls,
Enticed of drink he cannot buy,
Near some blurred window that outrolls
What lures hot thirst through avid eye—
How light the differences that lie
Between this idling sot and him
Who courts the drunkard's death where trim
Attendants wait, in club-rooms fine,
With walls and floors of rich array,
And pour from crystal flasks the wine
That helps him hurl his life away ! . .
Or yet the pale worn girl you see
Go hurrying with her bundled work
To them whose niggard wages free
Her days from penury's worst irk—
How easy amid that chestnut hair
And in those tired eyes' wistful gaze
Where stars inalienably dwell,
To mark the beauty a ball-room belle
Might nurture with unceasing care

For fashion's poor brief hour of praise! . .
What touch of foppery may we note
In this mere tatterdemalion's air
Who sticks a dropped flower in his coat,
A rusty hat-brim sideways tips,
Winks gaily, and smiles with unshorn lips,
And shows that through some grave mischance
In evolution's onward flow
By nature he was born a beau,—
This rowdy of random circumstance! . .
Or, yonder, watch the itinerant wag
Extol his trumpery curbstone ware
With copious words that never flag,
As witty as they are debonair.
What embryo orator is there!
One push, and destiny's dark hands
Had lifted him to shine elate
In senatorial debate,
The idol of constituent bands—
Not then, as now, with railleries rank,
The street-boy's peddling mountebank!

Even thus, in countless ways like these,
Resemblances, analogies,
Loom clear between the limits twain

Of rich and poor, of toil and ease,
Of bitter need and bounteous gain.
Alas! that equal sunbeams rain
Sweet largess on all men alike,
While men themselves to ruin strike
Those bonds of kinship that should bind
Their race in one consentient kind!

MEMORIAL VERSES.

TO COURTLANDT PALMER.

Howe'er we speak of death as of an end
Whose pale oblivion touches all alike,
Still, when some sturdier man of help and use
Deserts the dignities he wore so well
And makes them seem like hollow garments flung
Where late they clad him fair in favored life,
Then those that here on earth have missed him most,
Whether to sadly doubt or strongly trust,
Say, as they grieve and dream, "There should have
 been
Some loftier and more honored exodus
For such as he, so lifting him elect
Above this cold democracy called death!"

But no; the impartial shears of Atropos
Cut with the same twin blades each mortal strand.
Death has no privilege, no preëmption, no
Allotment, appanage, prerogative.
Over one narrow threshold, with nude feet,
The mightiest or the meanest pass and fade.
Yet always there are gifts the dead may leave

The living, and as I muse on him we mourn,
About the pathos of his absence, rise
Columnar memories, like the marble art
That clothes a temple; for he sought to find,
If rightly I judge, amid the turbulence
And hurry of our brief days, a trysting-spot
Wherein all theories, creeds, philosophies
Might with harmonious intercourse convene,
And win, by mutual tolerance, as time fled,
That wisdom intellect alone may reap
From the fair tree of knowledge, when we slay
Its worm of prejudice that gnaws the root.
"Come, all," he said, with invitation sweet,
With clarion hospitality, "come, all!
Taste this new liberal sacrament that brooks
Believer, Deist, Pantheist, Atheist, Jew,
And blend in comradeship about its board!
Ye men of church and ritual, guard your tongues
From too impetuous fervors of defence.
Remember that the Christ ye so adore
Was guiltless both of spleen and arrogance!
No hot polemics fumed in Galilee;
No peevish ironies of pulpiteers
Blared rancorous from the 'Sermon on the Mount.'
Ye men that bow to Science as your god,

Learn self-control and patience from her laws.
Remember Newton and Copernicus
Killed superstition with the sword of truth ;
They did not scare it dead with rhetoric.
Hysteria never framed a syllogism,
And logic murders like a gentleman."

So did he speak, this gatherer of the clans
From many a vale and hill of human thought.
Alas ! his falchion and his plaid are now
But silent relics in the lonesome hall
Of recollection.   Yet his energy,
His charity, and the incomparable zeal
He kept undaunted in our service, live.
Such tender immortality as his,
Material in these unforsaking friends,
Throws challenge at the skeptic's hardiest doubt.
To-night we are all believers ; here, for once,
The agnostic pleads no ignorance of our theme ;
A common faith in one high work and wish
Binds us together.   May the sanctity
Of such communion pass not from our souls,
But nerve us, in the future, with new force
To ply the unfinished purpose he began !

Read at the Nineteenth Century Club, November, 1888.

IN THE YEAR TEN THOUSAND.

(Two citizens meet in a square of the vast city, Manattia, ages ago called New York).

FIRST MANATTIAN.

Welcome. Whence come you?

SECOND MANATTIAN.

I ?   The morn was hot ;
With wife and babes I took the first air-boat
For polar lands.   While huge Manattia baked
Below these August ardors, we could hear
Our steps creak shrill on dense-packed snows, or see
The icy bulks of towering bergs flash green
In the sick arctic light.

FIRST MANATTIAN.

Refreshment, sure !
How close all countries of the world are knit
By these electric air-boats, that to-day
Seem part no less of life than hands or feet !
To think that in the earlier centuries
Men knew this planet swept about her sun,
And men had learned that myriad other globes
Likewise were sweeping round their myriad suns,

Yet dreamed not of the etheric force that makes
One might of motion rule the universe;
Or, if they dreamed of such hid force, were weak
To grasp it as are gnats to swim a sea.

SECOND MANATTIAN.

They dreamed of it; nay, more, if chronicles
Err not, they worshiped it and named it God.
We name it Nature and it worships us;
A monstrous difference! . . This light fountain
    plays
Cool in its prophyry basin; shall we sit
On this carved couch of stone and hear the winds
Rouse in the elms melodious prophecies
Of a more temperate morrow?

FIRST MANATTIAN.

As you will. (*They sit.*)
Watch how those lovely shudderings of the leaves
Make the stars dance like fire-flies in their glooms.
It is a lordly park.

SECOND MANATTIAN.

In truth it is.
And lordliest this of all America's
Great ancient cities; yet they do aver

That once 'twas fairly steeped in hideousness.
The homes of men were wrought with scorn of art,
And all those fantasies of sculpture loved
By us they deemed a vanity.   I have seen
Pictures of their grim dwellings in a book
At our chief library, the pile that hoards
Twelve million volumes.   Horrors past a doubt
Were these dull squat abodes that huddled close
One to another, row on dreary row,
Whit scarce a hint of our fine frontages,
Towers, gardens, galleries, terraces and courts.
They must indeed have been a sluggard race,
Those ancestors we spring from.   It is hard
To dream our beautiful Manattia rose
From such uncouth beginnings.

FIRST MANATTIAN.

You forget
The city in their dim years, as records tell,
Was but a tongue of island—that lean strip
Of territory in which to-day we set
Our palaces of ease for them that age
Or bodily illness incapacitates.
Then, too, these quaint barbarians were split up
In factions of the so-named rich and poor.

The rich held leagues of land, the poor were shorn
Of right in any . .   I speak from vague report ;
Perchance I am wrong.   Manattia's ancient name
Escapes me, even, and I would not re-learn
Its coarse tough sound.   In those remoter times
Churches abounded, dedicate to creeds
Of various title, yet the city itself .
Swarmed with thieves, murderers, people base of act,
So that the church and prison, side by side,
Rose in the common street, foes hot of feud,
Yet neither conquering . .   Strange it seems, all
    this,
To us, who know the idiocy of sin,
With neither church nor prison for its proof.

SECOND MANATTIAN.

I, too, have heard of lawless days like these,
Though some historians would contend, I think,
That fable is at the root of all events
Writ of past our fourth chiliad—as, indeed,
The story of how a man could rise in wealth
Above his fellows, by the state unchid,
And from the amassment of possessions reap
Honor, not odium, while on every side
Multitudes hungered ; or of how disease,

If consciously transmitted to the child
By his begetter, was not crime ; or how
Woman was held inferior to the man,
Not ably an equal ; how some lives were cursed
With strain of toil from youth to age, while some
Drowsed in unpunished sloth, work being not then
The duty and pride of every soul, as now,
Nor barriered firm, as now, against fatigue
With zeal sole-used for general thrift, and crowned
By individual leisure's boons of calm.

FIRST MANATTIAN.

You draw from shadowy legend, yet we know
That once our race was despicably sunk
In darkness like to this crude savagery,
Howe'er the piteous features of its lot
Have rightly gleamed to us through mists of time.
From grosser types we have risen by grades of change
To what we are ; this incontestably
We clutch as truth ; but I, for my own part,
Find weightiest cause of wonder when I note
That even as late as our five-thousandth year
(Though fifty-millionth were it aptlier termed !)
Asia, America, Europe, Africa,
Australia, all, were one wild battle of tongues,

Nor spoke, as every earthly land speaks now,
The same clear universal language.   Think
What misery of confusion must have reigned !

SECOND MANATTIAN.

Nay, you forget that then humanity
Was not the brotherhood it since has grown.
Ah, fools ! it makes one loth to half believe
They could have parcelled our fair world like this
Out into separate hates and called each hate
A nation, with the wolf of war to prowl
Demon-eyed at the boundary-line of each.
Happy are we, by sweet vast union joined,
Not grouped in droves like beasts that gnash their
    fangs
At neighbor beasts,—we, while new epochs dawn,
Animal yet above all animalism,
Rising toward some serene discerned ideal
Of progress, ever rising, faltering not
By one least pause of retrogression ! . .

FIRST MANATTIAN.

                 Still

We die . . we die! . .

SECOND MANATTIAN.

Invariably ; but death
Brings not the anguish it of old would bring
To those that died before us.   Rest and peace
Attend it, no reluctance, tremor or pain.
Long heed of laws fed vitally from health
Has made our ends as pangless as our births.
The imperial gifts of science have prevailed
So splendidly with our mortality
That death is but a natural falling asleep,
Involuntary and tranquil.

FIRST MANATTIAN.

True, but time
Has ever stained our heaven with its dark threat.
Not death, but life, contains the unwillingness
To pass from earth, and science in vain hath sought
An answer to the eternal questions— *Whence,*
Whither, and For What Purpose ?   All we gain
Still melts to loss ; we build our hope from dream,
Our joy upon illusion, our victory
Upon defeat.   .   .   Hark how those long winds flute
There in the dusky foliage of the park.
Such voices, murmuring large below the night,
Seem ever to my fancy as if they told

The inscrutability of destiny,
The blank futility of all search—perchance
The irony of that nothingness which lies
Beyond its hardiest effort.

SECOND MANATTIAN.

Hush ! these words
Are chaff that even the winds whereof you prate
Should whirl as dry leaves to the oblivion
Their levity doth tempt ! Already in way
That might seem miracle if less firm through fact,
Hath science plucked from nature lore whose worth
Madness alone dares doubt. As yet, I allow,
With all her grandeur of accomplishment
She hath not pierced beyond matter ; but who knows
The hour apocalyptic when her eyes
May flash with tidings from infinitude ?

FIRST MANATTIAN.

Then, if she solves the enigma of the world
And steeps in sun all swathed in night till now,
Pushing that knowledge from whose gradual gain
Our thirst hath drunk so deeply, till she cleaves·
Finality with it, and at last lays bare
The absolute,—then, brother and friend, I ask
May she not tell us that we merely die,

That immortality is a myth of sense,
That God . . . ?

SECOND MANATTIAN.

Your voice breaks . . let me clasp your hand !
Well, well, so be it, if so she tells.   At least
We live our lives out duteously till death,
We on this one mean orb, whose radiant mates
Throb swarming in the heaven our glance may roam.
Whatever message may be brought to us,
Or to the generations following us,
Let this one thought burn rich with self-content :
We live our lives out duteously till death.

(A silence.)

FIRST MANATTIAN.

'Tis a grand thought, but it is not enough !
In spite of all our world hath been and done,
Its glorious evolution from the low
Sheer to the lofty, I, individual, I,
An entity and a personality,
Desire, long, yearn . . .

SECOND MANATTIAN.

Nay, brother, *you alone !*
Are there not millions like you !

FIRST MANATTIAN (*with self-reproach*).

Pardon me !

(*After another longer silence.*)

What subtler music those winds whisper now !　.　.
'Tis even as if they had forsworn to breathe
Despair, and dreamed, however dubiously,
Of some faint hope !　.　.

SECOND MANATTIAN.

　　　　　　　I had forgot.　That news
The astronomers predicted for to-night !　.　.
They promised that the inhabitants of Mars
At last would give intelligible sign
To thousands who await it here on earth.

FIRST MANATTIAN.

I too had quite forgot ; so many a time
Failure has cheated quest !　Yet still, they say,
To-night at last brings triumph.　If it does,
History will blaze with it.

SECOND MANATTIAN.

　　　　　　　Let us go forth
Into the great square.　All the academies
That line it now must tremble with suspense.

A SLAYER OF POETS.

I HATE new poets? Well, and if I do,
Leave me to hug my hate; it's mine not yours.
Once I adored the whole soft-hearted tribe,
And treasured many a stanza writ by them
That now to read stirs nausea. I have sat
Aloof in my small attic at eighteen,
And watched the stars push early silver out
Above the city roofs, and with my pipe
Blurring stark chairs and bedsteads till they looked
Ideal for symmetry, dreamed Orient dreams
That mocked to-morrow's breakfast as a myth,
And turned the uncouth brick stable opposite
Into a Moorish mosque. Bah! poetry!
I loved it once as bees love hollyhocks,
As humming-birds love honeysuckle ; I've passed
Whole hours in yonder tramp-roamed park by night,
To note the summer fountain flowering there
Into mysterious petals of pale foam
Below the regnant moon. But work was work,
And mine dull drudgery with a pen of prose
That wrote those bald mechanic facts I scorned,

Yet dared not shrink from, since the task meant bread.
Then, later on, I married; scribes like me,
That scarce with decency can help one life,
Are sure to crave the helping of one more.
We clutch, we drowning men, at matrimony,
As though 'twere accident's fortuitous plank
The Islands of the Blest had drifted us.
Of course my bride was dowerless, and yet all
The diamonds of Brazil were not to me
Worth those two virgin amethysts, her sweet eyes!
I wrote more poetry in our honeymoon,
And afterward as well, when sturdier toil
Gave me a jealous interim.   Then chanced
Her motherhood. That made me think of prose,
For prose was knit to thrift, while verse, forsooth,
Murmured "starvation" as I wrought its rhymes.
More children came, and with them more demand,
Exaction, charge, responsibility,
And cold insidious disillusionment,
Till one day, fingering at a sheaf of songs,
I said: "They are only such red sparks as fly
From the iron on the anvil ere 'tis bent
Into obedience—brilliant chaff at best,
Not the big metal forged by blows of art,
Beaten and crushed by burly power to shapes.

Of beauty or majesty or delicacy.
" Why here's no poet at all," I told myself,
" But only a fellow that has witched his brain
Into the fallacy of seeming one—
Just as if some stray shepherd of Greek times,
Wandering a hillside where the laurels clung,
Had suddenly seen, grouped on a low slant cloud,
The awful Nine, with fillets and white gowns,
And afterward gone dreamy and strange of mood,
Himself more witless than his nomad flock,
Spoiled for a shepherd, yet elected not
To destiny divine as Ganymede's ! "
Well, brooding thus, I clenched a stoic's teeth
And flung those lyrics headlong in the fire.
They flamed from nothingness to nothingness,
Leaving my dead ambition in their dead
Ashes !   And now you tell me I am called
The slayer of poets ?   Not a name inapt.
Granted I write invective merciless
On each new poet that dares lift his head ;
The very vitriol that I choose for ink
Has heart's blood blended with its acrid flow,
For disappointment like to mine has bred
More critics like to me than ever yet
Genius made glorious bards of.   Mark you that !

PAUL AVENEL.

(*Coast of New England.*)

HOMEWARD from tropic seas he came, a sailor bold and
brown,
And saw the scarlet moonrise flame above the distant
town.

The locust gave him dreamy song, the breeze blew
fresh and free.
" O love," he thought, " it is not long ere I clasp hands
with thee ! "

A touch on his firm shoulder fell, a voice fell on his ear :
" Whence have you come, Paul Avenel, and wherefore
come you here ? "

He knows the face, though gloomed it be, the voice,
though sad, he knows.
" Luke Amyot, friend, if you are he, speak blither
words than those.

"Speak welcome warm and welcome gay. Do I not
need glad cheer ? "
Luke Amyot sighs and turns away. . . "You shall
not find it here ! "

Pale in the eerie light is Paul. "O say the truth," he
cries,
And louder than his language call the yearnings of his
eyes.

An answer sounds in broken voice : "The love you
held so true
Is worth no honest lover's choice, but treacherous unto
you !

"Look yonder where the lights illume that mansion
towering proud. . .
The bride was young and fair, the groom with weight
of age was bowed.

"He promised grandeurs manifold—the ancient heart-
less tale;
He bought her with a flash of gold, a costly wedding-
veil ! "

Paul Avenel in silence hears, in silence dark and
    stern ;
His deep eyes wear no trace of tears, but keenly,
    strangely burn.

"Luke Amyot, if I did not know," at last he gives
    reply,
"Your truth were stainless as the snow, these words
    would seem a lie !

"O trusted with a trust supreme ! O worse lost, in
    thy shame,
Than though I saw thy grave-slab gleam and read thy
    carven name,

"What curse from lips of mine can vie with anguish
    that shall make
My future one dead blank for thy poor despicable
    sake !"

He lifts a white face to the skies, he lifts a wrathful
    arm.
"Hold ! curse her not !" Luke Amyot cries ; "may
    God forbid such harm !

"For never lie more foul was told, I swear, than this
of mine !
Not all a kingdom's proffered gold could tempt her
love divine !

"And even in death her parting thought was your
sweet loyal slave ! . .
For now two April-tides have wrought fresh grasses
round her grave !" . .

Paul Avenel in silence hears, and slowly understands.
The low moon sparkles on his tears and gilds his
heavenward hands.

"Thanks, friend," he murmurs, "for the rude cold
lie that smote to save !
In grief and yet in gratitude I go to seek her grave !"

THE ASPIRER.

Two stars for ages had in counterpoise
Whirled their great globes about the same great sun,
He radiant in our night while viewless they,
Being planets lit of him, their system's lord.
Yet gloriously each flashed its borrowed beams
Back to their glorious giver, as each rolled
In rhythm and splendor through eternity.
Twin stars were these, if judged by interspace
Of heavenly distance, though they seemed as twin
Solely because close-blent they flamed afar
To orbs that mightier voids repelled and swathed.

Yet deeps of difference were between these twain,
Shining as either shone the satellite
Of its vast luminary, and drinking life
Sheer from his rays.   Both stars to throngs they held
Were full of mutable charm as earth is full,—
With wood, vale, mountain, lake and rioting sea,
Chill bourne or tropic, zone of ice or bloom.
Yet one star held a people in soul and aim
Less than earth's man at basest.   Right and law

Were palsied in its polity, and the toll
Ambition paid to power was coin of bribe.
Justice, with eyes unbandaged, bore no scales ;
Whole streets of towns were dense with droves of poor,
Whose lips wan famine made too weak to curse
The tyrannies cheating them of vital bread ;
Women were thralled and spurned there ; war at
   whiles
Flared its red torch and left sad mounds of slain
To mark the shadow it cast. The rich lolled sleek
In luxury, with their villas, gardens, groves,
Their games and wine, their lutes and dancing-girls,
Their pomps of vice, their raillery, languor, scoffs,
And their immeasurable fatigue. The star
Clear through its fair entirety reeked with ill.
Some spell malign had smitten it, and it swung
Piteous yet beautiful, through gulfs of sky.

Its mate for thousands of slow years had seen
The ignominy it shrined, and fervently
Had longed to stir by some celestial means
Of counsel its rank torpors of disuse.
Realmed in that sister star a race abode
So taintless that their lives, from death to birth,
Were snow for chastity, yet fire for love.

Honor and truth were daily breath to all ;
Woman with man had interchanged as boons
The traits of noblest worth in either sex,
Till vigor and sweetness, intellect and heart,
Authority and obedience, doubt and trust,
Met in one equal bond of husband, wife,
Sire, mother, son or daughter, and each note
Of kinship melted to a single sound,
Simple yet complex, tender yet sublime,
Humanity.   In their homes, as in their marts,
Labor was unison of want and help,
A glad democracy of mine and thine,
A scorn of greed, a reverence of self-rule.
Crime loomed a vague historic memory here,
Even as disease and war, pests fangless now.
Where ancient squares with palaces were flanked,
While forms of great dead poets engirt him, pale
In marble perpetuity, year by year
The living poet exaltedly would read
His lay to listeners whom its music stirred,
And often with rapture ; for though science illumed
Abysses of the unknowable and blessed
Their star with order, wisdom, peace, content,
Still, poesy had not swooned below the glare
Of fact, but ever wreathed in fantasy

The real, until ideal and real were knit
Like branch to leaf, or stem to flower. . . The
    calm
Of this clean perfect world was absolute.
Death bred no gloom, for death was long ago
Shorn of all pain or struggle, and sank on those
It lulled as ripeness on a falling fruit
That drops in dewy autumnal grasses, grown
So soft and ripe themselves you scarce may hear
The faint thin echo of its lawnward lapse.
To live was health ; to die the drowsy lease
Of sense, in drifts of throeless quietude,
With holocausts on pyres whence pitying flame,
Odorous as lustral, shot to heaven alike
Eulogium, epitaph and elegy,
And so wrought *requiescats* kindlier far
Than mouldering headstones of forgotten graves.

And yet to live meant splendid ease and range
Of search, desire and opportunity
Whereof we dream not save in flights of myth.
Forces that greet our ken by no dim guess,
Bowed their fond servitors ; all drink whose lure
Clouds the sane mind they loathed as hurt and bane ;
The food they ate was very marrow and pith

Of sustenance, yet no dumb creature bled
To sate their whims of appetite, but viands
For us ambrosial, though to them plain birth
Of chemic lore past earthly formula,
Nourished their needs; they swept o'ersea with speed
To us deemed fabulous; air had meekly told
The mystery of its ways to their winged ships.
They pored through visual glass of wondrous tube
On lands of other planets, noting there
Unnumbered forms of thrift or negligence,
But ever scanned most lucidly the globe
Nearest their own. The headlong sin of this
Wrung them with sorrow; it was the only blot
On their white happiness; a myriad eyes
Daily regarded that insensate sphere,
And in a myriad souls the wish had crept
To tell its habitants what sluggard wills
And nerveless aims on ruin had stranded them.
The pure star yearned to reach the faultful one;
Throbs of compassion urged this mood of help;
Through telescopes of power magnificent
Beside our optic effort when its force
Of mechanism hath no residual trick
To further map the moon, or test the gold
Smelted in Saturn's wizard rings, the star

Of good looked on the star of evil, and declared
Its fell degeneracy.   Pity there
Wept with a silent weakness that was worth
A warrior's brawn.   New decades came and wove
Elaborate schemes for intercourse, yet each
Being tested was found futile.   Still endured
In one star the desire to wake, warn, cheer,
Ameliorate ; and still in one endured
The dumb blind sensuous anarchy that made
Millions reel reckless from the paths of right.

At last the watchers thrilled with hope ; their craft
Aerial, that could leap to pierce the films
Of fleeciest clouds, had ever paused in dread
At loftier voyages.   Arctic bournes of naught,
Illimitable vacuum, feeding cold
As blood feeds flesh, had ever spread to them
Its menaces of blank discouragement.
Ether, an ambient ether, as they knew,
Prevailed through all creation, verging it
On multitudinous borders, like the wash
Continual of the same pervasive sea
Embosoming an archipelago.
And yet what keel of æronautic skill
(Long ancestors of their best brains had asked)

Were shrewd enough to dare such raw bleak wastes?
Must these not ever bide unnavigable?
Or, if some spirit of intrepidity
Heroic essayed their freezing amplitudes,
Must he not perish in dire strait ere half
The attainment of that stellar goal he craved?

And yet the watchers thrilled with hope at last.
For one among them, dowered beyond his kind,
A youth with limbs like sculpture hewn from light
And eyes that burned below the majesty
Of brows our Greece hath never given her gods,
Rose up and spake before a populace
That swarmed the imperial terraces and courts
Of the great statue-girded square.   His voice
Pealed in melodious eloquence, and rang
Nobility, candor, zeal, faith, sacrifice.
He swayed his hearers even as blast will sway
Ocean ; irradiate seemed his face to those
Tranced by the angelic ardor of its look ;
And while erelong with murmurs, hands upflung,
Smiles, tears, they surged by thousands close to him,
In protest of their lealty, thus he spoke :

" We all have seen the world we all would help ;
Its folly of degradation shields no crime

From our sharp quest ; yet its one aid is we.
Still, he who dares its frontier challenges
Death, but he dying, if die he must, shall live
Thenceforth in immemorial sanctity
Of honor for the races that shall press
Their footprints on his undistinguished clay.
No worthier wage could he or ask or seek,
This man who scorned himself to save a world.
For we have probed infinity to its last
Lair of the insoluble, and while we shrink
From all rash arrogance of postulate
Affirming no God is, have lost desire
To find God elsewhere than in godliness
Of duteous healthful days from birth to bier.
Long years ere now desire hath failed in us
For immortality that should mete so much
Paid bliss for so much virtue our side death.
The immortality we would win is here,
In deeds of unreluctant righteousness.
Our heaven is wide as human sympathy
May push her boundaries, folding them who stamp
On evil as them who faint in her fierce coils ;
Our hell is narrow as ignorance and fear,
Twin architects of ill, can fashion it,
With caves that mine the glooms of bigotry

And roofs that scoff the sun from rafters thick.
Our church is charity, our religion, love ;
The fanes we erect are wrought with masonries
Reason had learnt the skill of ; for she took
Hard plinths of truth and mortised each to each
With soil that bloody and tearful martyrdoms
Had soaked when superstition ruled, not she.
Hence they stand firm, and those that worship there
Glow the fanatics honesty begets,
With rite and ceremonial that are acts,
Not forms—benevolence and compassion, not
Their lazy reflex.   Friends, who deign to list
My utterance, I have shaped, or this I deem,
A peerless air-ship that shall strike its beak
Safe in the soil of yonder waiting world.
Its giant valves hide stores of element
Wherewith by bond of willing ducts to fill
The faint lungs through the lips that gasp.   Its weight
Hath nicety of deft alternation, now
A feather and now a plummet, as demand
Shall fix.   The voyage that I shall make with it
Taunts, if ye will, destruction.   Yet to die
Aspiring thus I rate a glory above
All fruits of triumph that a soul may win
While honor points the road that safety guards.   .   .

O friends, your beating hearts beat time with mine !
This in the enkindled looks that leap to me
I note and treasure.   Would your hand-clasps all
Were concentrate in one, so I might gain
Sweet multiplicity of encouragement
Merged in a single fervor of farewell !''

He ceased, and tumult roared response to him,
With plaudits volleying from impetuous throats.
Legions flocked nearer, crying and kneeling ; some
Caught at his robe and kissed it ; some held up
Their children, that his image might remain
Regnant in memories of the little ones
When they themselves were silence ; women tore
Flowers from their breasts and flung them at his feet ;
The statues of the great dead seemed to rock
In the great square below this turbulence
Of acclammation, while o'er all a sky
Like hollowed amethyst framed a huger sun
Than ours, with lordlier disc and ampler blaze.

The morrow of this most fateful day beheld
His embarkation on the venturing ship.
Throngs met once more, to mark his going ; and now
The elation they had shown but yesterday

Had vanished wholly ; a stillness born of awe
And mixed with melancholy in place of joy
Reigned on each visage as it ruled each mind.
But he, the undaunted aspirant, strong son
Of bravery and self-abnegation, smiled
His bright exultance on the gathered mass,
Then turned, and with an athlete's vault of ease
Lit on the pendulous deck of his weird bark,
Tethered beneath yet softly oscillant
In the bland air that buoyed it.   Wide it loomed,
A thing of tenuous frailty for the sight,
But through its delicate branchwork of contour
Slept energies mad tempests could not drain.
No captain, helmsman, sailor, save himself,
Guided the vessel ; he, companionless,
Went journeying forth upon the infinite.   .   .
A moment, and he had cut the cords that bound
His quivering argosy ; it shot aloft
Like some miraculous bird, and following it
Rose a long cry, that echoed on for years
Through histories of the people whence it sprang.

Fleetly the ship sped upward ; but ere dusk
They scanned it well through many an optic glass
Whose lenses had wrung secrets from their night.

They saw the audacious mariner of heaven
As clearly as if he plowed some neighbor sea.
All could not gaze, but those who saw not heard
Of his unfaltering courage, and the tact
Wherewith he had ably governed rope and sail.

" His face is like a deity's," they avowed.
" He feels no fear ; none ever yet hath scaled
So dizzy a height above us, yet he stands
Without one glimpse of tremor. . . Look, he waves
A hand to us whom he no more discerns ;
For knowing of how we still discern him, still
He signals. . . Hail to him, grand soul ! "

Night fell, and drowned him from their view. Till
     dawn
Vague hordes held sleepless vigil, some with hope,
Some with despair—with fierce anxiety all.
But when at last the whitening orient drove
Gloom from the lustrous labyrinths it paled,
They sought their first dim chance to peer again
At the high resolute ship. . . And then a moan
Of sorrow arose that seemed to touch and stay
The conduits of the fountains of the morn.

For now they saw the ship, in ruinous plight,
Plunge, veer, wheel, battle, as if some hate unseen
Clenched it, while he that strove to man it leapt,
In terrible pathos of unquelled resolve,
From prow to stern through flurry of tattered sails
And tangle of flying cordage.   .   .

                                    Then they saw
Hope fade from out his face. " Lost ! lost ! " they
      wailed.   .   .
Many drew shuddering from the sight, and bowed
Their heads in anguish. . . Those that yet stared on,
Averred long after that his countenance,
Just ere the steep death snatched him whence he
      soared,
Was worth a life to have witnessed ; so serene
And holy it beamed, and so divinely proud,
Even at the instant of his overthrow.

            *   *   *   *   *.   *

Ages have passed since thus he dared, thus died ;
Yet on the star he rose from towers a tomb
Statelier than all the monuments it rears.
His bones rest here, say some, but others claim

His downward body in that stupendous fall
Turned vapor, and so vanished meteor-like. . .
And yet what matter if tomb or cėnotaph ? . .
Among its clustering turrets the four winds
Flute requiems, and below, in lichened stone,
The unobliterated legend lives :
"*No mortal ever failed who strove as he.*"

REVERIES.

I.—A TULIP-BULB.

With care I scanned it in a wintry hour,
  As though my steadfast look would search for signs
Of that mysterious transfiguring power
  Whose charm its dull rotundity enshrines.

What hidden strength could dower this torpid plant
  All sublety of conjecture dared not guess,
Chill, callous, earthy and insignificant,
  Engirt with husks of swarthy brittleness.

But now, when mellowing April's mirth or tears
  Fill heaven with sweet caprice of storm and calm,
I watch how radiantly its outgrowth rears
  A gorgeous chalice, brimmed with fragrant balm

*   *   *   *   *   *

Ah, little maid, beneath my window there,
  Disdained by hurrying passers while you ply,
With ragged garments and with tangled hair,
  Your shabby broom that keeps the crossing dry,

Of you, poor weary starveling, who shall say
　What beauty and fragrance might not break control,
If love's dear luminous warmth once found its way
　In through the dark of your neglected soul?

II.

O swan, what memories rarely sweet
　To your white majesty belong,
While in this public park you meet
　The stares and gapes of many a throng?

In willowy grace and stainless hue
　Your regal curves are yet akin
To that sleek beauteous bird which drew
　The enchanted car of of Lohengrin.

And while your charms my look enchain,
　Sweet visions through my fancy float . . .
I see some delicate châtelaine
　Feed you beside some castle-moat.

Or when bluff barons lolled at wine,
　In far mediæval midnight hours,
I see you where the moonlit Rhine
　Wound glittering under dusky towers,

While there, in pale mysterious plumes,
  Till daybreak fired the ghostly skies,
You weirdly swam through dreamy glooms,
  With maddening songs and women's eyes.

St. James's Park, 1889.

III.—IN MID-OCEAN.

How could the Greeks make Love be born of thee,
In whose cold spaces love could no more dwell
Than sorrow in youth, or joy amid a knell,
O bleak and uncompanionable sea !
Nay, stirred with ire and hate in like degree,
Now swollen as when we see a snake's throat swell,
Now wreathed as when his body its wrath would tell,
Thy wandering waters ever form and flee !

Sweet is thy tremulous bosom, richly clothed
In light that leaps or loiters, beams or broods,
And sweet thy toss, thy glory, or music grave ;
Yet ah ! who ever knew thee well but loathed
The vast blank circuits of thy solitudes,
The treachery coiled below thy brightest wave ?

  At Sea, 1884.

IV.

WHILE the broad night above me broods,
In all her shadowy plentitudes,

I let my roaming vision fare
Through many an aisle of starry air.

"Bright throngs," I muse, "that o'er us bend,
How vague the messages you send !

"That fiery star, within whose rays
A wicked blood-red ardor plays,

"May be some world where dwell serene
A race with souls divinely clean !

"And this large tear of saintly light,
O'er the dead sunset throbbing white,

"Its snowy splendors looking now
Fit for some aureoled angel's brow,

"This star through ages may have been
Some great wild world gone mad with sin !"

V.—A SQUIRREL.

WHERE yonder stately chestnuts, blent in one,
Hide cool aerial archways from the sun,

You roam on agile feet, in furry guise,
With bounteous wisp of tail, black beads of eyes.

Though colored like the inert brown branches' hue,
The spirit of their light leafage lives in you!

And while you gambol amid their breezy dark,
Fantastic reveller, with delight I mark

The alert shy head, the nimble leap and pause,
The chattering voice, the restive click of claws,

The idyllic ecstasy, the buoyant power,
The elusive grace, until you seem, this hour,

Like some strange wingless bird, whom Heaven has lent
A shadowy forest for its firmament!

VI.

DEAR lavish blossoms that light the Junes,
        And fold our fields with the tender haze
        Of those pure petals that grow like rays
From the downy rims of their golden moons,

Pale throngs that the suave wind ripples through
  With the placid surges of sleeping lakes,
  Bright largess that fresh young summer makes,
In her sweet wise way, out of morning dew,

O daisies, dainty and coyly prim,
  When I watch you blooming I always seem
  To be wandering back, in a drowsy dream,
Where the meadows of childhood glimmer dim !

The meadows that manhood sees no more,
  The meadows of story and of song,
  Where little Red Riding Hood trips along,
To knock at her grandam's cottage-door !

Where the ghost of Bo-Peep goes roaming, too,
  And seeks her flock while she rubs both eyes,—
  The meadows where elfin echoings rise
From the phantom horn of Little Boy Blue !

The meadows of innocence, mirth and rhyme,
  Lying far aloof from the world's wide din,
  The bounteous meadows that never have been,
Yet will always be, till the end of time !

VII.—AN AUTUMN DAY.

WHEN dawn breaks chill the birds are still—
   Not a wee numb throat that twitters   .   .
And meshed in the grasses, pearl on pearl,
   The marvelous hoar-frost glitters.

The sun rides up, and the hollyhock's cup
   Has lost its crimson wassail,
And the poppy stirs a ruined crest,
   And the corn a bleaching tassel.

A sharp wind tears the pippins and pears
   Off branches, onward sweeping ;
The blue plums drop, and the ivory gourds
   Through wilted leaves are peeping.

O'er meadowy ways there floating strays
   A silken fleece of thistles,
And the swarthy chestnut's yellowing husk
   In lane and pasture bristles.

To a sound of sighs the fair year dies,
   And the brief day waxes older,
And every gust that strips the pomp
   From the gaudy wood is colder.

Now twilight falls, and the chamber walls
Grow dim, and the white stars glisten,
And out in her gloom the katydid calls
For lonely hearts to listen !

VIII.

SOMEHOW I have lived without you
    All these years ;
Never dreamed a dream about you,
    Felt no fears ;
Neither missed you nor required you,
Had you not, nor yet desired you.

I have dealt with mirth or mourning,
    Day by day,
Loving, hating, prizing, scorning,
    Man's old way.
This would charm or that would cheer me ;
Life was life, and you not near me !

Well, the months were measured duly ;
    I drew breath.
It was life.   Ah, truly, truly,
    Life, not death.
Yet such life as lacked the giving
Of one grace to make it living !

IX.

I FEEL the huge dim city round me lie,
Still drugged with sleep below the whitening sky.

Now sounds the sluggish roll of distant wheels ;
Now falls the unsteady step of one who reels.

For year by year, in strange weird trysts like these,
Meet toil and vice, the intense antitheses.

But save for such chance noise amid the air,
A deathly and solemn calm is everywhere.

Deep in my soul, this ghostly dawn that springs
Fresh from eternity, speaks awful things !

Here to my side she seems, with spectral dress,
To steal like some pale mighty prophetess,

And tell me in some vague mysterious way
How o'er the shadowy roofs the speeding day

Inexorably bears within its breath
New joy, despair, sin, anguish, birth and death !

X.—To a Reformer.

Nay, now, if these things that you yearn to teach,
  Bear wisdom, in your judgment, rich and strong,
Give voice to them, though no man heed your speech,
  Since right is right, though all the world go wrong.

The proof that you believe what you declare
  Is that you still stand firm though throngs pass by;
Rather cry truth a life-time to void air
  Than flatter listening millions with one lie !

XI.—Grass.

The rose is praised for its beaming face,
  The lily for saintly whiteness ;
We love this bloom for its languid grace
  And that for its airy lightness.

We say of the oak "how grand of girth !"
  Of the willow we say " how slender !"
And yet to the soft grass, clothing earth,
  How slight is the praise we render!

But the grass knows well, in her secret heart,
   How we love her cool green raiment,
So she plays in silence her lovely part
   And cares not at all for payment.

Each year her buttercups nod and drowse,
   With sun and dew brimming over;
Each year she pleases the greedy cows
   With oceans of honeyed clover.

Each year on the earth's wide breast she waves,
   From spring until stern November;
And then she remembers so many graves
   That no one else will remember!

And while she serves us with gladness mute,
   In return for such sweet dealings
We tread her carelessly underfoot,—
   Yet we never wound her feelings!

QUEEN CHRISTINA AND DE LIAR.

GLAD the day that saw Christina, broad of brain though
    young in years,
Take the crown of glorious Vasa, girt with Sweden's
    proudest peers.

Regal was the face they looked on, regal were the form
    and guise,
Regal were the light-blue lustres of her Scandinavian
    eyes.

"She will rule us," cried the people, "like her sire,
    Gustavus great ;
War at·this girl's frown shall thunder ; peace upon her
    smile shall wait.

"Yet below her kingdom ever, civic wisdom, patriot
    love
Shall be pediments majestic to the monument above !"

Time with happy confirmation proved the praise whose
    welcome strain,
Like an archway for a conquerer, spanned the thresh-
    old of her reign.

Ten bright years her lifted sceptre loomed in power
  o'er land and seas ;
Norway, Prussia, Denmark, Austria trembled at her
  calm decrees.

Battle in righteous loathing held she, yet no dastard
  armistice made ;
Half Minerva, half Brunhilda, Sweden's destiny she
  swayed.

Oxenstiern, the astute old statesman, oft her might of
  mind would own ;
Grotius, poet and historian, laid allegiance at her
  throne ;

Torstenston, the unrivalled soldier, served her with his
  valiant men ;
Blunt Salmacius, wily Vossius, flattered her with tongue
  and pen ;

Keen Descartes, who grandly brooded on the spells of
  time and space,
Lost his learning in the sorceries fashioned by her
  virgin face ;

Milton, he whose thought was earthquake to an age of
    sloth and swoon,
Praised her as the lark the morning, as the nightingale
    the moon.

Many a suitor sought her favor; princes hotly vied
    with peers;
Magnus Gabriel de la Gardie urged his cause with
    smiles and tears;

Uladislaus, King of Poland, tried her maiden heart to
    thrill;
Spain's fourth Philip strove to tempt her with alliance
    loftier still.

But alike entreaty or protest ineffectual found her
    mood;
She was adamant to all men, howsoever subtly
    wooed.

Yet would sages, wits and pundits, bards, philosophers
    and priests
In her palace at Upsala throng to share her stately
    feasts.

Here, one evening, 'tis recorded, lights in plenteous
    measure played,
Through the imperial apartments, on a mirthful mas-
    querade.

And of multitudes assembled, none so lured the royal
    glance
As De Liar, the Chevalier, jovial, handsome, fresh from
    France.

He, like all except Christina, wore a mask of envious
    fold,
Yet the Queen, through secret signal, his identity had
    told.

Speech urbane her lips addressed him; radiant looks
    on him she bent;
Other suitors, keenly watching, gnawed their beards in
    discontent.

" 'Tis the Frenchman," they would whisper; " fortunate
    he should be wed,
Else perchance our bold young sovereign by some wild
    caprice were led."

Later, when the night grew merrier, when the feasting-
hall was gay,
Stealthily De Liar glided to a chamber yards away.

Here, where old Norse gods were pictured on the
drapery's fold and flow,
Glided stealthily to meet him a mysterious domino.

From a face of blooming witchery soon its mask of
velvet fell;
The Chevalier stood confronted by the wife that loved
him well.

"'Come," she laughs, "my wandering gallant, say me
frank and say me fair!
Have you left your heart entangled in the Swedish
Queen's gold hair?"

Laughing back with amorous ardor, the Chevalier
makes reply:
" Nay, already in your brown tresses doth my heart
entangled lie!"

" Flatterer!" mocks the wife—but kisses all her raillery swiftly choke,
Fond as those that lily or poppy may from buoyant
bee invoke.

" Fear not, lady of mine," he murmurs, " lest new love
  your rights profane ;
I to this crowned Queen am colder than the frost-
  flowers on her pane !

" Pettier is her dull self-worship, fed by parasitic
  prate,
Than the crowd of salaried pedants truckling to her
  trivial state !

" Hers a royalty to reverence ! Nay, we witnessed,
  you and I,
Our own lordly and gracious Louis on his white stairs
  at Versailles !

" Hers, forsooth, a court of splendor ! Nay, we saw, in
  other years,
Those great pomps that made the Tuileries one pale
  blaze of chandeliers ! "

Thus he spoke, far less of slander than bravado on his
  tongue,
Spoke, nor ever dreamed how deeply his audacious
  words had stung.

For with blue eyes glittering icy, with fierce wrath in
    all her mien,
Near at hand, behind an arras, cowered the unsus-
    pected Queen ! . .

In the heaven of royal favor, slowly from that fateful
    night
Rose the star of the Chevalier, sweeping up to
    haughtier height.

Military rank was given him ; orders gleamed upon
    his breast ;
Often at Queen Christina's table he would sit a welcome
    guest.

Soon his poor wife pined and languished ; faith and
    hope were rudely wrecked ;
Snared by dizzying dreams of greatness, he had galled
    her with neglect.

Wherefore, now, when supplications and remonstrances
    had failed,
Equally in scorn and sorrow back to her own land she
    sailed.

The Chevalier, to detain her, strove at last with strong
dismay,
But she had learned what potent magic in the Queen's
least whisper lay.

" I will share his love," she murmured, while the dark
ship spread its wings,
" With no other living woman, be she born of churls
or kings !"

So to France the sad wife journeyed ; and ambition's
greedy flame
From the conscience of De Liar banished his remorse-
ful shame.

Through the future's mist that mantles every deed our
spirits dare,
He beheld a shadowy sceptre, waving beckoning in the
air.

On it ever seemed to tempt him, till there came a
pregnant hour
When he almost felt his fingers clasp it with impetuous
power.

Once again while sumptuous revels turned her palace
    halls aglow,
Did the Queen upon De Liar copious blandishments
    bestow.

"Now," they said, "he nears the summit of his
    insolent success;
Every glance Christina gives him hides and harbors a
    caress."

"He to-day is virtual Regent; in his name large
    mandates meet;
On what giddier grade of lordship may to-morrow land
    his feet?"

While in babbling throngs they gossiped, the Chevalier
    drank his fill
Of that dangerous wine Christina could so craftily
    distil.

Through the dance beside her suitor moved she with
    august repose;
Now her eyes were melting sapphires, now her lips an
    opening rose.

Once, by hardier courage prompted, in her ear he dared
    to sigh :
" Since Diana loved Endymion, wherefore did she let
    him die ? "

Low he leaned to catch her answer ; but it came in
    loitering tone :
" Turn your metaphors more nicely. . . 'Twas
    Endymion's fault alone ! "

Flushed the infatuate young Chevalier while he
    thought : " Perchance she means
My divorce were given for asking by the priests that
    cringe to queens ! "

But aloud he breathed : " Be piteous, O my lady of
    light and grace ! " . .
" Look," she smiled, " our last cotillion. . . Come,
    Chevalier, take your place ! "

In the dance, like one delirious, near the Queen he
    paced and bowed,
Till her clear voice clove his spirit as a moonbeam
    cleaves a cloud :

" I depart . . yet seek me later at my boudoir's
  private door. . .
Take the long south gallery leading past the sculptured
  bust of Thor.

" Fear no guards ; I have dismissed them ; none will
  wait to watch or snare. . .
They that are most wise at hoping prove but dullards
  at despair."

Through the lane of bending courtiers fled Christina
  from his look ;
Off his mind its trance of rapture slowly the Chevalier
  shook.

Soon along the wide south gallery did he move with
  cautious mien,
Reached the door, unclosed it lightly, crossed its
  threshold, met the Queen.

Now his heart beat fast and furious while upon his
  knees he fell. . .
" Rise," Christina suavely faltered ; "such allegiance
  is not well.

"If indeed your love's large fervor from your soul
    confession draws,
Bravely speak it like a soldier, though a Queen hath
    been its cause!"

"Oh, my sovereign, my enchantress!" leaping to his
    feet, he cried;
And he flung both arms about her, drunk with passion
    and with pride.

But Christina darted shivering from the strenuous
    embrace.
"Do you love me?" rang her answer. "See how such
    love brings disgrace!"

Then she shrieked "Help! help!" and straightway,
    as responsive to her need,
Guards and gentlemen-in-waiting filled the room at
    breakneck speed.

"Hear me, all!" proclaimed Christina. "He, the wretch
    that yonder stands,
Dared profane our sacred person with his sacrilegious
    hands!

"Like a thief he sought our chamber, yet with wish
　　more wild and bad ;
We should deal him death immediate, did we not
　　believe him mad !"

" Mad ?" the assemblage loudly echoed, though in
　　dazed and wondering style ;
" Mad ?" the poor Chevalier shuddered, awed by such
　　abysmal guile.

" Mad, indeed !" shot back Christina, "yet some pity
　　attends our scorn.　.　.
To the mad-house at Upsala let him instantly be
　　borne !"

　　　*　　　*　　　*　　　*　　　*　　　*

Five slow years of stern immurement followed as De
　　Liar's doom,
Till the new King, Charles Gustavus, loosed him from
　　his living tomb.

But at last he hailed his freedom with no greetings
　　warm and glad ;
Misery, self-reproach and bondage had in good truth
　　made him mad.

Back to Stockholm soon he drifted, and in beggary
  spent his days,
With his face of ravaged beauty and his memory-
  haunted gaze.

And he oft would say to passers, like a man of wandering wit :
" Can you tell me where's my country ? I have lost
  my way to it ! "

      *   *   *   *   *   *

Who recalls not how Christina threw aside the crown
  she wore,
Roaming other lands of Europe, joyed to be a queen
  no more ?

Strange the fortunes that befell her, bright or sombre,
  harsh or sweet. . .
All remember Monaldeschi, dying suppliant at her
  feet !

Oft her name was dipped in odium, till her people, far
  aloof,
Learned to clothe it with the colors of perpetual re-
  proof.

Feared alike for plots and scandals, now in Paris, now
    in Rome,
Tired at last she grew of exile, and bethought herself
   of home.

Not a trace of tribute met her till old Nórköping she
    gained ;
Here, through many a dismal streetway, night with
    desolation reigned.

Northward faring, past the frontier she as monarch had
    surveyed,
Wroth she grew that sullen silence over all the land
    was laid.

"What ! " she fumed ; " no troops, no escort ! Every
    window dark as fate !
Fickle Swedes that once adored me, has your love so
    soon turned hate ? "

But the words thus framed in anger died upon her lips
    in fright,
For a glimmering apparition dawned that moment on
    her sight.

Round about the royal carriage giddy and volatile it
    sped,
And the starlight showed it vaguely, like the resur-
    rected dead !

Back the snow-white hair blew ghastly from a face of
    idiot leer,
As it tossed its antic tatters, whirling there and wheel-
    ing here.

" Look," it cried, " the great She-Spider to her web
    hath crawled again !
Bolt the portal, bar the casement, Swedish maids and
    Swedish men !

" Bar the casement, bolt the portal ! Lie ye still and
    give no sign,
Lest she suck the blood from your heart as she sucked
    the blood from mine ! "

        *   *   *   *   *   *

So Christina, home returning (fame, love, power one
    cold eclipse !)
Found the mockery of this welcome from the mad De
    Liar's lips !

CAPRICE.

(A Certain Mood of a Certain Mind.)

It is so supremely odd,
I must laugh, in spite of spleen.
Here I am, a sort of god,
In a temple purely mine,
Having worshipers who mean
Right obeisantly, no doubt,
Going in and going out,
With their raiment rich and fine ;
Going up the marble stairs
In their trios and their pairs ;
Coming, going all the year,
Just to pay me homage here.

I cannot help but laugh,
It is so superbly queer
That I, with more by half
Than my wildest wish could choose ;
With my costly rubbish, got
Anywhere, one might say,
From Lapland to Cathay ;
With my glass, a hundred hues,

And my grand books, and my lot
Of antique gems, pure, unflawed.
And my enviable huge hoard
Of pictures,—and untold
Money behind it all,
With a name whereto such old
Memories of riches cling,
That when spoken it seems to ring
Like a sudden blow on gold.

It is so acutely strange,
One is forced to laugh, you know !
Yet for me the chill of change
Is like bare feet plunged in snow.
Now, were she some great dame,
I should smile, and let it pass ;
But a little low-born lass—
Why 'tis utterly not the same !
A mere street-girl, who sells
Buds and violets in the square,
(With two waves of red-gold hair
Over black-lashed purplish eyes)
A poor slight girl, who dwells
In some attic, on coarse fare,
Yet who placidly repels

The chance of queenlike ease,
And to breakfast, if she please,
On a pearl, Cleopatra-wise !

It is so intensely quaint,
I must laugh, in spite of pride.
To see my power defied
By this reedlike frailty here !—
To get her dauntless " no "
From this unexpected saint,
This problem in calico,
With a few scant loaves a year,—
Who dares in one life, thus,
Be hungry and virtuous !

It is so uniquely droll,
It will end I know not how.
For when a man like me,
Who has never learned till now
What thing it is to be
Thwarted in any need—
With whom desire is goal
Already unto deed—
When a man like me shall say
" I wish," and find all ways
But one strait single way

Baffling intention's greed,
Then it should not much amaze
If he set his teeth and cried
With imperious headlong ire,
"'*Tis enough that I desire;*
I will not be denied!"

And so, my little lass,
Vending violets in the square
(With your black-lashed purplish eyes
Under waves of red-gold hair),
Since it thus should come to pass
That I waste all this immense
Self-believed omnipotence
On a weakness that defies,
Refuses, and at length
Seems a citidel of strength—
Should it therefore wake surprise
In the world that I despise,
If I took that one strait way,
If I .   .   married you, some day?

SUB ROSÂ.

(*Paris : Second Empire.*)

SHE is quite the queen of the town
　Since he married her, three years since,
　He, near of kin to a prince
Who narrowly missed a crown.

A terrible match, on my life!
　The old prince looked dark for days.
　Then, quite on a sudden, he pays
High court to his kinsman's wife.

'Twas her beauty that did it all,
　And her mellow voice, and her style
　Of letting that mobile smile
Lie just as her sweet lips' call.

She came from . . Heaven knows where ;
　From Heaven itself, some said,
　With her stars of eyes, and her head
Folded over by shining hair.

And now, in her new grand life,
　She is free from the worst tongue's blame.
　No slander assails her name
Of spotless woman and wife.

And the vanquished old prince, they say,
  Makes her state just so much more grand
  By bending to kiss her hand,
In his portly and courtly way.

* * * * * *

Now I chance to know and be sure
  That this woman's rich robe is borne
  Each week up a stair forlorn
Of a certain dwelling obscure.

And in a dull room where she peers,
  Is a child (having just her sweet face)
  That she clutches with fierce embrace,
And low little moanings, and tears.

Then down the dim stair she will go,
  And gaining the street, glide out.
  She would have that child killed, no doubt,
If 'twere not that she loved it so! . . .

How the past in its look must speak
  (Half her shame and half her delight!),
  While she hides it here out of sight,
Stealing up to it once a week!

And the world, which is now her slave,
  How little its laugh would spare
  If the ghouls of scandal could tear
That past of hers from its grave!

ANACREONTIC.

(From the French of Théophile Gautier.)

O POET, do not fright my love
　By ardor's too impassioned flame,
Until it flies, a timorous dove,
　And leaves me bathed in rosy shame.

The bird that through the garden sings,
　Before the least vague sound will flit ;
My passion, that is dowered with wings,
　Will vanish if you follow it.

Mute as a marble Hermes cold,
　Below the arbor linger here,
And from his bower you shall behold
　The bird descending, without fear.

And soon your brow shall near it feel,
　While breezy waftures charm the sense,
A fluttering of soft wings that reel
　In white aerial turbulence.

And on your shoulder, tamely meek,
　- The dove at last will perch in bliss,
And quaff with his pink balmy beak
　The dizzying rapture of your kiss !

PAUL HAMILTON HAYNE.

(Died July 13, 1886.)

REARED from the race unfaltering hope endows
    With happier lore than rigid reason shrines,
      For you, dead friend, midsummer tamely twines
The exequial wreath to rest on those pale brows !
You should have died with airy and dulcet vows
    Of mating birds in April shades and shines,
      And when the glooms of your dear Georgian pines
Had flecked with furtive green their feathery boughs !

For as the earlier dews of Spring will throng
    Bright on some flower that gives to breeze or bee
      Its delicate symmetries and fragrant breath,
Even so, for years, clung shining round your song
    The certitude of immortality,
      The faith in resurrection after death !
August 30, 1886.

JACYNTH.

JACYNTH her name—a strange one, was it not ?
I thought so, I, frail girl that knew her born
While the young mother panted life away,
There in those calm hills by the Shenandoah.

When they had buried that sweet mother-shape,
It looked as if my master would go mad
For grief. . . I reared the babe.   He scarcely
    knew
If yet 'twere live till it was one year old.

We blacks were all slaves, then.   My master owned
But me and twelve stout others, men that tilled
His acres, few yet rich.   I, Lydia, spoke
As whites do, a quadroon, no common slave.

They said my master was my brother born ;
I never knew nor cared.   Whate'er he was,
He raised me above ignorance.   I was taught
From books, and treated with all kindliness.

Horrors of slavery ?   Yes, the whole South reeked,
I doubt not, with dark evils worse than pest.
But I and they that served with me were cloaked
In mercy.   Fierce tales reached us ; we were safe.

I never mated with black man or white ;
Straight on for years, while sweet Miss Jacynth grew
From child to girl, I watched her innocence
Break into maidenhood, like bloom from bud.

The first fierce grief gone, master changed his mood.
He treasured Jacynth (let me drop the " Miss ";
It wears a sound so cold, so far-off, now !)
Prizing her tenfold more than he had shunned.

She conned her lessons at his knee.   Her face,
Her smile, her touch, her step, was dear to him
As any wavering cloud that stooped in drouth
To damp the dry slopes of our thirsting hills.

I think such large affection never lived
Between two souls as that which now brimmed theirs.
He was her comrade, playmate, guardian, friend ;
She drank his thoughts, and paid the draughts in love.

For hours they roamed the woodsides, hand in hand ;
At eight she claimed his saddle in long rides ;
At twelve she spurred her pony near his horse ;
At seventeen, mounted fine, she shared his hunts.

One day, while she was yet of tender age,
My master said to me in private talk,

" Lydia, no word of heaven or hell, of creeds
Or heresies, must my Jacynth ever hear.

" I bade you even ere now say naught to her
On themes like these.   Have you obeyed me well ? "
I answered, " Yes, I have obeyed you well,"
But added, " Master, she has learned of death."

" How could she help," he sighed, "but learn of it ?
Still, 'tis my wish that she should look on death
As only on slumber that we all erelong
Shall find, and fold us with, like some soft gear.

" Pain, she will see, is oft the prickly stem
Whence death, a white and opiate flower, is born ;
The stern stem wounds us when we pluck the flower,
But from those petals pale we drink dear sleep.

" I shall live long ; 'tis in me to live long ;
But when I am dead she will inherit me.
No love shall vex her of a stormier sort
Than filial.   Peace will smile on all her days.

" For look you, Lydia, we are girt with calms
Of solitude among these healthful hills.
The town is far from us ; no man her peer
In birth or culture will behold her face.

"Unwedded shall she live; unwedded, die;
And dying unconscious of those turbid ghosts
That throng the doors of death—void wills-o'-the-wisp,
Mere shadowy dross of human fears and dreams—

"I do believe her lot will far transcend
For joy the usual one earth's millions meet.
So shall I pluck that single soul at least
From many an anguish countless hearts have known!"

. .   The war, a dim red spark of fire, gave threat
Of greatening, yet long steadfast bode. . .   At last
Our valley and mountains felt its heat and scathe.
My master left us, then, one blaze of wrath.

In his first fight he fell; the tidings drove
Through Jacynth's bosom like a bayonet-thrust.
But rallying after swoon and apathy,
She let her own sweet strong youth work its will.

"Lydia," she said to me, "though he is gone,
He gets the eternal peace in lieu of breath.
Surely 'tis better.   Can we mourn those dead?
Think of it, Lydia!   Infinite repose!

"Yet I do mourn his absence bitterly!
Still, soon . .   who knows if I, too, may not share

That same serene oblivion he gains now?
And yet to have seen him once ere housed in dust !"

Her tears flowed bounteous while she clasped my neck;
For on the battle-field where he sank slain,
That day of hideous rout and massacre,
His corpse with others lowlier was confused.

Found not, perchance 'twas mangled so none knew
The dear familiar features.   Yet, if seen,
What comfort?   Happier that he dwelt with her
Forever thus in memory, sound and hale !

"Good Lydia," soon she urged, "the negroes all
Have left us.   Can we bide here and not starve ?
I have kindred in the North—my mother's blood.
Let us go seek them; help me; do not thwart."

Why should I thwart her, I, a slave, who loathed,
The land that brought me bondage ?   Long ere this
I would have fled but for the vigilant love
She kept forever live within my soul.

We passed the lines, by trick, by shrewd disguise—
We reached the North, and after journeying sore,
Came to her Northern kindred.   These were two,
An old man, hard as flint, a grey gaunt wife.

Their home, a square cold prim New England house;
Their greeting, frost; their hospitality,
A truce between amazement and contempt.
Still, they allowed us lodgment; this we prized.

We prized it, being worn out with strain and fret.
But soon the wife warned Jacynth: "You must meet
Our minister, a reverend godly man.
Tell us what faith you practiced in the South."

"Faith?" murmured Jacynth, and her eyes' dark stars
Beamed wonderingly on mine. . . "She had no
    faith,"
I answered for her. . . "What! no faith?" shot forth
Her kindred, wife and man, in one fierce breath.

"None," said I.   "She was reared with gentlest care;
Her heart is full of love to all hurt things,
A wounded bird—yes, even a smitten worm—
But worship, church, religion, she hath none."

Then I told more.   They stared at me aghast.
"What pagan has our kinsman made of her!"
Stammered the wife.   And with applauding frown
The husband groaned, "Oh, sinner ripe for hell!"

"Hell? What is hell?" cried Jacynth, while her
  cheek
Faded as if in fear of some strange threat.
"We'll teach you if we can!" the woman piped;
"We'll teach you if our Lord wills!" fumed the man.

They taught her. Summoned from his pious lair,
The pastor of the village-flock drew nigh.
He droned to her for hours his laws of creed,
He filled her breast with tremors, doubts and glooms.

A kindly and earnest soul, this minister;
Yet ere a week he had so dulled and chilled
My darling that her sweet face gleamed to me
Drawn with strange pain, as though life stung her hard.

"Good? But I'm good, I, Lydia, am I not?
And this meek man, with voice all tender tones,
Has told me first of some great power he names
God—then he has told of this god's wrathful hate."

"Not hate," I ventured. "There is Christ, they say,
The son of God, who came to save the world ——"
But here I paused, remembering what I swore
To my dead master ere fight smote him cold.

"Christ? Yes, he spoke of one more merciful
Than God. . . Ah, Lydia, but he scared me so,

With all his curious talk of things beyond death ! "
She clasped me close with wild arms.   "*Is* it true ? "

" Have *you* not thought it true ? " I answered her,
And kissed the pearly cheek so lovingly
Laid near my duskier one.   She started back,
With terror glittering from her eyes' chaste calms.

" True ?   No !   And yet he is wiser than am I,
This minister they call the ' man of God.'
But think what father taught me of death's boons,
Its rest, its beauteous exodus from care ! "

How could I answer, then ?   My heart was wrung.
And *her* poor heart—they wrung it worse than mine !
They peopled it with phantoms, visions, fears ;
They stormed a heaven upon it, flared a hell.

Believe them ?   Why, they dazed her into that.
They left her with no force to disbelieve.
'Twas all so piteous !   Death had meant to her
Serenity, and they made it fierce turmoil !

They shocked her with the sin she might have sinned ;
They pierced her with the sin she must have sinned ;
They awed her with Jehovah's threat and curse ;
They stained her white peace with the bleeding Christ.

I dared not tell her to disdain their words
And seek the old contentment, shorn of dread.
I think they would have driven us out to starve
Had they even dreamed I would so spoil their aims.

Yet I beheld her frenzied with dismay,
Horror, sharp fright of self.   She oft would cry :
" Oh, Lydia, am I then so steeped in guilt ?
Why did this God make evil, he being good ? "

Or yet again : " If God hath meant us fair,
Why should he trip us with desires to sin ? "
Or yet, " If Satan be God's furious foe,
Why should Omnipotence not crush him dead ? "

Or still : " How can this God be merciful,
Seeing the souls he wrought with his own hands
Writhe on in flame for all eternity ?
Oh, Lydia, who could love a God like that ?

" Nay, give me back my heavenly dream of death,
Where no heaven enters, nor a dream of hell,
Nor any memory of earth's pain or bliss,
But all is one large long forgetfulness ! "

Then would she stare at some blank point of space,
As though an eye were in it, or a voice.

Ah, 'twas so piteous to behold her thus!
I felt her strained heart reel while pressed to mine!

And all this time her kindred watched us close—
The flintlike man, and she, his grey gaunt mate.
They flooded her with texts and parables;
They drowned her in their sermons, maxims, prayers.

I went to them, one day, and begged their grace
Of kindlier dealing.   With her acid mouth
Firm-set, the wife repelled me; with brows dragged
In scowl above lacklustre eyes, her lord.

What meant I?   Would I plunge the girl in doom?
Was not *I* Christian?   They had thought we slaves
Were piety to the bone.   So I, too, shared
The shame of my dead atheist master! Pah!

I flung myself before them.   " Do not heed
My piety or impiety," I beseeched.
" Think only of her, dear Jacynth, whom I love!
Think only of her who never bore till now

" This weight of ponderous wonder and suspense!
I know her delicate nature!   It will break
Below the burden that you load it with!
Your stern stress of religion comes too late!"

"Too late?" they shouted. "There is always time
For sinners that repent! We'll save her yet!"
Then the gaunt wife with one fond bony arm
Girt her lean lord. (Their childless bed was plain!)

They saved her—yes, they saved her! Baptism came
Hard on conversion's heel. Their village-church
Was packed, one morn, when Jacynth, paler grown
Than the white gown they clad her in, came forth.

A stubborn soul—and yet she had found at last
Salvation! Gently did the minister
Dip her frail form in so-called sacred bath. . .
I waited, quick to change her dripping garb.

But ere I had changed it she went mad, poor child!
There in my arms dear Jacynth raved and shrieked!
She called on Christ to cleanse her of vile stain ;
Then screamed " He will not hear!" deliriously.

Shuddering, I clasped her. All that day she raved,
Calling her father from the sweet cold sleep
He had taught her so to trust in—calling me,
"Lydia, dear Lydia!"—though she knew me not.

Toward night her glazed eyes melted into tears,
But still with pale and quivering mouth she cried:

"Father, come forth from your deep sweet sleep—
    come !
Take me to lie beside you and get peace !"

I love to think that he who loved her so
Came to her, took her, laid her down by him.
I love to think this, for at dark you died,
My Jacynth ! . . She that tells this tale lives on.

AFRICAN BALLAD.

" O Zanza, daughter of Zanzoor, quit plaiting of thy
    reeds ;
Come forth from thy dim-glimmering hut, bedight with
    plumes and beads.
For now thy father's warriors wait, drawn up in dark
    array,
Till blood-red on their naked limbs the rising moon
    shall play."

" O Nolki, nurse, O trusted nurse, what need have I
    to go
Where ruddier than the rising moon a brave man's
    blood will flow ?
Nay, tell my sire that here in peace his daughter plaits
    or spins,
And vainly shall he sound for her his drums of serpent-
    skins."

" O Zanza, daughter of Zanzoor, obey thy father's hest!
For though of all his hundred wives thy mother pleased
    him best,
His wrath at such rebellious words, from even such lips
    as thine,
Might shear thy tongue off at the roots and cast it to
    the swine."

"O Nolki, nurse, this fair strong man, with eyes of
    heaven's own blue,
Doth statelier stand beside our braves than oak beside
    bamboo ;
Yet they to-night, with toss of spears, with maniac leap
    and shout,
From his true breast, our gods to sate, would tear his
    true heart out !"

"O Zanza, daughter of Zanzoor, this bright-haired
    stranger came
With warriors warlike as himself, to whelm our land in
    shame.
His comrades all save him are slain ; alone he waits,
    this hour
(Chief offering at the moon's full dawn), to please the
    Moon-God's power."

" O Nolki, nurse, thy speech is false ; he fared as friend,
   not foe ;
He did but come our mystic lakes, our shadowing hills
   to know.
My sire's grim welcome to his band was meaner in its
   might
Than when below some hurrying heel some snake's
   quick fang will smite."

" O Zanza, daughter of Zanzoor, thy dusky cheek is wan;
Pray all the gods, thou king-born child, to shield thee
   from this man !
For though they rend his frame to shreds at rising of
   the moon,
His memory still may haunt thy life as gnats the sultry
   noon."
                          .

"O Nolki, nurse, his heaven-blue eyes have searched
   my heart so deep
It keeps their radiance like that flame the hearts of
   fireflies keep !
To burst his bonds, where prone he lay, my longing
   soul was fierce
As when the storm's pale javelin strives the empurpled
   cloud to pierce ! "

" O Zanza, daughter of Zanzoor, what harsh cries meet
　　mine ears?
The Moon-God shall his victim lack when blood-red he
　　appears !
Nay, plait thy reeds no more, dear girl, for clamoring
　　thousands hie
To tax thee with a traitorous crime thou dost not dare
　　deny ! "

" O Nolki, nurse, I do not fear; I brake the captive's
　　thrall ;
He gave me one warm kiss for thanks—one warm kiss
　　—that was all !
Far hence at this late hour he speeds from hungering
　　death's embrace.　.　.
O Nolki, nurse, with glorious joy I greet death in his
　　place ! "

A DIALOGUE.

BELIEVER.

THIS man of reason, whom you deem so great,
Who puts out Hell and bars up Heaven's fair gate,
Who flings all creeds terrestrial to one maw,
Huge as the Aztec battle-god's, called Law,—
Who makes the universe, to suit his wish,
As eyeless as a subterranean fish,—
Last night this valiant doubter, in his pride,
Shrieked for Jehovah's pardon ere he died.

INFIDEL.

With ease the partisan may falsely view
Delirium's rant; yet if indeed 'twere true
That some wild fear *did* seize him at the last,
What matters? Hardiest oaks are bowed by blast.
The warrior minds of men drink strength for strife
Not from death's opiate, but the elixir, life.
His life being great, who cares if near its close
He druled what imbecilities death chose?

LYRIC INTERLUDE.

I.

You tell me, friend, that seeing how fate has said
 The vetoing word which bids my footsteps fare
  No longer where elysian meadows lie,
  'Twere worthier wisdom than to yearn and sigh,
Hereafter with meek earthward-bended head
 To walk below the burden I must bear.

And then you promise that in days to be
 The love which I in stoic mood resign,
  Smitten with self-denial as with a sword,
  Shall pass and perish of its own accord—
Shall drop as drops the dead leaf from the tree,
 The o'er-luscious cluster from the vine.

Oh, friend, and while your quiet counsel gives
 This that you deem sweet comfort to appease,
  The inexorable truth you have not guessed!
  Learn that the heart within my desolate breast
Shudders to choose between alternatives ·
 Harshly unequal as are these !

Oh, learn that I would count it bitter gain
 To have been thus lightened of the bond I wore !

For I would rather sorrow long years through
Than lose the right to sorrow as I do !
Rather love on, though love were life-long pain,
Than suffer not, yet love no more !

II.—A Graveyard.

BENEATH no arch of earthly skies
    It lies ;
The long luxuriant grasses gleam
    From dream ;
The headstones, white as grief's white cheek, are
        wrought
    Of thought ;
With incorporeal emerald round its graves
    The willow or cypress wards and waves.

No human dead once treasured dear,
    Sleep here ;
But here a life's ambition knows
    Repose ;
Here a life's friendship (warm and fond, of old !)
    Rests cold ;
And here a life's poor slain love buried dwells
    Below phantasmal immortelles !

III.—In Poverty.

My one poor candle sputters,
　　My feeble firelight wanes;
The north-wind bangs my shutters
　　Against the frosted panes.

When the bitter night was younger
　　I craved bread in good truth,
But now I feel hard hunger
　　Fret me with iron tooth.

And while I shiver, keeping
　　This ghastly vigil here,
Across my soul is creeping
　　A fancy wild and queer.

I tell myself that hiding
　　In some far reach of earth,
Girt with dense dark, is biding
　　Some diamond of vast worth!

IV.—LOW LIFE.

LET your soul put on rags to-night ; we are going where
    life is low ;
Not, I mean, where murder will smite, not to dens that
    with thieves o'erflow ;
Not to haunts that shall shock, distress ; but to low life,
    nevertheless !
For caste hath lairs packed with pride not of righteous
    deeds but of race,
And avarice hath slums where bide the misanthropies
    that debase—
Though in either the rich light falls between grandeurs
    of gilded walls.

———

Nay, the outcasts not all may be found among alley-
    ways noisome with dirt ;
There are paupers unclean, unsound, whom penury's
    harms may not hurt ;
There are lives wealth-defended from ill, yet whose days
    are one poverty still !

V.

THE year was dying, the wind went sighing,
   The leaves were flying on many a gust.
At day's last splendor I saw them render,
   With reverence tender, dust unto dust.

From earth upmounded the first clod sounded;
   My sad heart bounded with pity deep
For him forsaking the light and taking
   This cold unwaking eternal sleep!

But closer gazing, my soul amazing
   Past power of phrasing, I marked, erelong,
That she, his nearest in life and dearest,
   Wore brow the clearest of all that throng.

And while I wonder, as dull clods thunder
   On him whereunder the worm shall grope,
O'er that low coffin, anon and often,
   Her sweet lips soften with smiles of hope.

And half in spurning, half, too, in yearning,
   Yet envious-burning, my soul avers:
" No king could measure all earthly pleasure
   Against the treasure of trust like hers!"

VI.—To E. N. C.

(Died at Oxford, England, January 4, 1875.)

I KNEW thee not amid those sunnier times
   When wealth and homage waited thy command,
When youth and flattery mixed their festal chimes,
   And life went singing lightly, lute in hand.
I knew thee only when thy soul was sore
   From bitter loss and tired with earthly din,
And when thou stoodst upon a twilight shore
   To watch the wrecks of hopes come drifting in.

And oh, 'twas sweeter to have known thee thus !
   Through sundering years thy picture still to praise,
Dear as the echoing of some *angelus*
   Whose music floats from unforgotten days !
To have seen thy placid fortitude, and how,
   The wearier that thy wounded spirit grew,
As many a one wears halcyon roses, thou
   Didst wear thy sad rosemary and thy rue !

To call thee friend was far more precious gain
   Than half the accomplished aims of men's desire,
Patient where others would have moaned for pain,
   Gentle where others would have flushed with ire ;

Tender in charities to all thy race,
   Mild, courteous, kindly, sympathetic, good,
Dowered with culture's most alluring grace,
   And matchless in devoted motherhood !

For me, when others mocked my distant goal
   As shadowy fancy of an idle boy,
Thy counsellings fell sweet upon my soul,
   Like holiest benedictions, bringing joy ;
And thine the inspiring word that gave me heart
   To watch with gaze more steadfast and more strong,
Far in the blue unsullied heaven of art
   The elusive and upwavering wings of song !

So now, o'er wastes of alienating sea
   I make my farewell as a bird to fly,
And eastward wandering, pause at last by thee,
   To linger near thy grave, but not to die.
For if the summer's mellowing smile shall set
   A single flower above thy sleep, I trust
Downward through this to thrill with my regret
   The dumbness of thine irresponsive dust !

VII.

THE clouded east was fiery-creased where the late moon
    mounted up ;
The frost hung white on the garden box and white on
    the poppy's cup.
As a faint wind woke in the autumn oak, the sere
    leaves earthward fell,
And harshly the wrangling katydids called through
    the misty dell.

Unrestful grown in her grave alone, she had left its
    midnight gloom,
She had crossed the churchyard's rimy sward from
    gleaming tomb to tomb.
With not a sound o'er the sodden ground of meadow
    and road she came,
And saw from the garden paths beneath the moonlit
    windows flame.

Sad-faced and wan, she glided on ; she neared the
    darksome porch,
Where flashed in the faded clematis a fire-fly's dizzy
    torch.

No summons heard, no hinges stirred, as mortal guest
 were there,
She slipped along the shadowy hall and clomb the
 silent stair !

And now her tread beside his bed paused in the
 chamber dim ;
A pitying moonbeam touched his head ; she stooped to
 gaze on him.
And at his side the youthful bride lay sleeping pure
 and fair,
With folded hands upon her breast, as though she
 dreamed a prayer.

From brow to throat a glory smote the bridegroom's
 placid face ;
She searched it long but only found content's benignant trace.
"The years have brought new joy," she thought ;
 "the mourning-hours are done.
Back to thy tomb in the cold and gloom, thou pale
 night-wandering one !"

VIII.—A BLACKBERRY IDYL.

Two graceful shapes, they moved at morn
  Through grass that scarce had lost its dew,
And where, keen-girt with many a thorn,
  The beaded berries darkly grew.

And while they leaned to pluck the fruit,
  And talked of love, as maidens please,
One voice was like a merry flute,
  One plaintive as an autumn breeze!

At last with heat gay Fanny cried :
  " You starve your soul on hope's poor crust."
And gentle Elsie softly sighed :
  " I only love because I must!"

But now a man's deep murmur said :
  " No other love is worth the name!"
And Fanny laughed and lightly fled,
  But Elsie lingered, thrilled with shame.

He bent her fluttered hand above,
  He pressed it close, in fervent wise,
This brown young farmer of her love,
  With golden beard and winsome eyes.

  *   *   *   *   *   *

When Elsie, in an hour and more,
  Came homeward to her father's farm,
The little basket that she bore
  Was almost empty on her arm.

But Fanny ran to meet her, here,
  And said, with eyes whence laughter shot,
"Your basket may be empty, dear,
  But oh, I see your heart is not!"

IX.—PIGEONS.

PINK-FOOTED, sleekly white or delicate fawn,
  Or darklier plumed, with glossy throat where clings
  One soft perpetual ripple of rainbow rings,
How often to your beauty our sight is drawn
When back from roamings wide you suddenly dawn,
  A dainty turbulence of fluttering wings,
  And light on some brown slanted roof, like Spring's
Pale showers of blossoms on an orchard lawn!

You haunt our barnyard life, plain, stolid, rude,
  With tender purity it is dear to note,
    And innocent gladness blithe as morning dew,
In many a long and mellow interlude
  Through homelier sound serenely letting float
    The smooth luxurious music of your coo!

X.—A Dead World.

Oft when I gaze on the clear moon's full round,
  Reveries amid my spirit form and float
  Of how unaltering in her orb remote
One icy annihilation broods profound.
Yet radiant life may there have thriven renowned,
  With intellectual aims of noblest note,
  With patriots, heroes, men that ruled or wrote,
With progress widening to thought's utmost bound.

But now, poor moon, wan shadow of your past pride,
  You bear a look like some pale glorious flower's
    When treacherous autumn wakes with poignant
      breath,—
Forever lifting, while slow centuries glide,
  Above this live and populous earth of ours
    Your silence, pallor and apathy of death !

XI.—For a Book of Light Rhymes.

Come, volatile Folly,of the roguish eyes
  And locks blown refluent from fair mirthful face,
Come, brilliant in your bell-besprinkled guise,
Come, delicate as the first shy rose of June,
  With childlike upcurled lips and dancing eyes,
With helm-shaped jingling cap and scarlet shoon.

Come forth and wake the indolent echoes well,
  With many a random burst of reckless glee,
With tinkle of wrist-bell and of ankle-bell,
With clear insatiate song and laughter bold!
    Thou red-lipped romp, come forth, I charge of thee,
Come, chide the old weary world for growing old!

For oh, 'tis a world of yearnings and of tears,
  A world of labor and death and chilling loss!
And rarely enough the parsimonious years
Give heartsease, and full oft unsavory rue;
    And many a frail back bears a heavy cross,
And many a sweet bloom dies for lack of dew.

But better if we laugh blithely now and then,
  Turning upon the past sad memory's key;
Ah, better in truth, worn women, weary men,
Than waste an hour with grief, regret or spleen,
    Watch this mad Folly of mine, in songful glee,
Pirouette beneath her ribboned tambourine!

XII.—ENVIRONMENT.

THIS earth, where so mysteriously we came,
  Girds us with kinships: in robust oaks dwell
  Our fortitudes; the willow and fern too well
Our foolish frailty or pliancy proclaim;

The dawns are our pure deeds ; the erratic flame
  Of lightning flares our passions ; the grave spell
  Of moonlight speaks our sorrow—and scarce we tell
Our pictured lives from their terrestrial frame.

Wherefore, the closlier that we lean to look
  On those material and yet airy ties
    Which bind us to this orb through fated years,
We almost feel as if great Nature took
  Our joys to make her sunshine with, our sighs
    To weave her winds, and for her rains our tears !

XIII.—DEATH'S PLAINT.

I DREAMED of Death, a maid with spotless gear,
  With slumberous eyes, with bosom warm and deep
  As though some tired head there might sink to sleep
In rapturous rest unflawed by one least fear.
" Oh, surely," I said to her, " no cause were here
  For all the eternal terrors that o'ersweep
  Humanity, and that oft so whelm and steep
Its last weak hours in torment so austere ! "

"Ah, true," with pale and beauteous lips Death
      grieved ;
  " I bring man but the oblivious boon he needs, . .

Yet note thou my dim realm where cypress waves;"
Then following her sad gesture, I perceived
The myriad spectres of man's own void creeds,
That crawled like haggard ghouls among his graves!

XIV.

Ho! for Dreamland's happy harbors!
Who's for Dreamland, by the ferry?
Who's to breast the waves that bind it,
Breast the fairy waves and find it,
Rich in flowering groves and arbors,
    Though the boat's a timorous wherry
And the sailors, vague in features,
Are the shadowiest of creatures?
Ho! for Dreamland! Heigh! for Dreamland!
    Who's for Dreamland, by the ferry?

Here are scholors pale with musing;
    Revellers that no more are merry;
Maids whose loves were empty anguish;
Lovers that for life must languish;
Patriots passionately choosing
    All the old haughty hopes to bury;

Sculptor, painter, bard, musician,
With unreached ideals elysian   .   .
These for Dreamland! those for Dreamland!
   Straight for Dreamland, by the ferry!

Off they push, and out they wander,
   Faring fleetly toward the very
Midmost heart of that great curly
Cloud that roseate and yet pearly
Haunts the dubious distance yonder,—
   Bound where blossoming sprays of cherry,
Apple, and all sweet trees are vernal
With a plenteous pomp eternal!
Ho! for Dreamland!   Heigh! for Dreamland!
   Halcyon Dreamland, by the ferry!

XV.—METEORS.

How strangely through the immense unclouded gleam
   Of shadowy skies, to solemn calmness given,
Flash out these hurrying golden lights that seem
   The wild aerial accidents of heaven!

Silent as blossoms that in odorous Mays
   Fall at the tremulous breeze's mild caress,
Down dim serenities of night's awful ways
   They float mysteriously to nothingness.

But while in volatile beauty speeding so,
   They touch the infinite with scarce deeper trace
Than if some languorous hand should vaguely
    throw ·
   A glimmering lily through the dusk of space.

Along its measureless purple, densely-starred,
   No answering tremor wakes, or faintest noise ;
Eternally by these mishaps unmarred,
   Reigns the cold radiance of its equipoise.

Even thus, one after one, the friends we prize
   Drop from life's maze when the ordained hour
    shall doom,
Closing at last their dulled indifferent eyes
   And journeying forth amid unfathomed gloom.

Yet when they are passed, at fate's commandment signs,
  Too often, against the darkness death shall weave,
Their memory's brightness perishably shines,
  Like those pale furrows that the meteors leave !

HOW A QUEEN LOVED.

I.

(THE QUEEN AND BLONDIVAL.)

THE QUEEN.

'Tis dear to think that in this isle I rule
The people's loyalty should steadfast bide
As yonder heaven that curves one cloudless blue
Above the crags and myrtles of my shores.

BLONDIVAL.

They love you for your father's martial name;
They love you for your grandsire's arts of peace ;
They love you—Shall I count the ancestries,
King, queen, prince, duke, that make them love you
    so ?

THE QUEEN.

Is that then all ?

BLONDIVAL.

        Nay, since they worship you
For your immaculate self.

THE QUEEN.

Immaculate ?
Those words ring mockery, husband.   Pray recall
How I had sworn to wed no man, but stay   ·
Sovereign yet virgin, ere we met and loved.

BLONDIVAL (*kissing her hand*).

Your people are dumbly ware such love as ours
May scale the stars, nor keep one touch of earth.

THE QUEEN.

Are they so wise, my people ?

BLONDIVAL.

Ay, Majesty,
With you for sweet instructress !

· THE QUEEN.

Nay, my lord,
Humility and not majesty for thee !
Have I not given thee all, my Blondival ?
Has not my soul to thine been bee to flower ?
Oh, there are times when I turn sick for loss
Of passionate prodigalities my love
Would heap on thy dear life !   This Blondival

Sits reveller at my board whose meats and wines
Are trivial to the scope of his true meed.
What fresh choice dainty on what rare golden dish
May I, his eager handmaid, serve him next?
How thwart satiety with new zest and tang
Of delicate savor?   Would that I might mix
Taste, music, perfume, color, charm of touch
Into one ecstacy of sense for him!
Yet no; I am powerless to delight him more;
I can but stand his vassal, though his queen.

BLONDIVAL.

One thing thou couldst give yet thou wilt not give!

THE QUEEN.

Oh, Blondival!   Again that piteous plaint!

BLONDIVAL.

Piteous, and yet unpitied!   Were thy love
The self-surrender thou assertest it,
Thou couldst not overbrow me day by day.

THE QUEEN.

I overbrow thee!   I that am thy slave!

BLONDIVAL.

Splendid inded a servitude like thine !
Humbly thou cringest that with nod of head
Couldst fling me seaward from thy steepest cliffs !

THE QUEEN.

My royal consort !

BLONDIVAL.

        Phrase that emptier sounds
Than scream of gull or crackle of autumn leaf !
I royal consort, whom thy furthest kin
Waive and precede at every public pomp!
Why, even the common oaf that plows and plants,
Lord of his own hearth, my superior looms.
Keep thou thy crown ; give me thy woman's robes,
Don these of manlier make ; and so attired,
Prove me thy "royal consort" in good faith !

SYLVIA (*singing outside, with lute*).

O the ways of love, O the ways of love,
    They are stern, yet soft as dew !
O the days of love, O the days of love,
    They are light, yet darkness too !

THE QUEEN.

(Less light than darkness, bird-throat, as I live!)
Look, Blondival, I have given thee all save this
Obvious co-rulership; yet such void boon
Still dost thou crave, though barriers built by law,
As oft I have told thee, crowd upon thy wish.

BLONDIVAL.

Barriers the state has wrought.

THE QUEEN.

      Hence all their might.

BLONDIVAL.

The state is thou.

THE QUEEN.

     Three centuries ere I breathed,
Our canons barred the sovereign of this isle,
Woman or man, from vesting in a mate,
Though even of kingly blood, equality.

BLONDIVAL.

Bad governance grows brittle enough to break
After three centuries have aged it so.
Snap such mere rottenness by one bold wrench
Of the wrist, and stamp it to oblivious dust.

THE QUEEN.

If thou, dear love, shouldst bid me die for thee
In testimony of passion, I believe
All nature, from her star of utmost bourne
To her least meadow-flower, did I rebel,
Would seem to taunt and pierce me with rebuke.
Yet this entreaty of thine doth none the less
Break futile on that faith heredity
Hath seared and melted into mind and soul.
My life I am free to give, but not my throne,
Bastioned and hedged with sanctity of trust.

BLONDIVAL.

So be it.   I shall not plead with thee again,
But strive to make the husband in me chime
Harmonious with the lacquey !

THE QUEEN.

Blondival !   .
I thought thy love would wiselier school itself
To patience with my one dissentient mood.
But mark: for thee, so worshipfully held,
I waver in compromise, and grant this grace :
Till three moons hence thou rulest in my stead,
From sole to finger-nail a regnant king.

The throne is thine—inalienably thine—
Through just that term of days, which once being fled,
Again thou shalt become Duke Blondival,
My king, yet not my nation's.   Dost consent?

BLONDIVAL.

Regent for three months .   .   .

THE QUEEN.

Nay, king absolute,
With me for subject.   Here's my royal hand.
Ere fall of sun the isle shall ring with it,
And he that dares deny King Blondival
May bow in heartier homage to cold steel.

BLONDIVAL.

I do consent.   (Three months of reinless power!
Oh, Sylvia, how I long to tell it thee!)

SYLVIA (*entering, abashed*).

The Queen . . .   Duke Blondival?   .   .

THE QUEEN.

Nay, Sylvia mine,
History has altered since we saw thee last.

I'm Duchess Blondival, more crownless, child,
Than thou, with that fine glory of gold silk hair.
And here's our King. Come, do him reverence.
Kiss thou his hand first ; I will follow thee.

II.

(Blondival and Sylvia.)

BLONDIVAL.

She keeps her word. The people adore her so
They bear even this magnificent caprice
As though 'twere some slight change of mode at court,
Gaudier insignia, deeper bend of head,
The delicate heightening of a shoe-heel—Pah !
I curse her when I think what sway she keeps.

SYLVIA.

Hush ! These dim faces on the tapestries
Look as though listening when your speech flows thus.
Oh, God ! a few weeks gone, and I do think
It would have turned my blood ice had I heard
The Queen's name used except obeisantly !

BLONDIVAL.

There is no Queen. She hath been dead two months ;
Would Heaven one more month raised her not to life !

SYLVIA.

How can you hate her when she loves you so?

BLONDIVAL.

I do not hate her, Sylvia, yet she bars
My reach from two dear purposes—thyself
As queen, her throne to reign on at thy side.

SYLVIA.

My spirit was not shaped for regal shows;
I have the violet's meekness in my blood.
Perchance 'tis therefore that with dark bold brow
And will imperious thou hast so enthralled
This frailty and softness born thine opposite.

BLONDIVAL.

Oh, Sylvia, men with turbid souls like mine,
Vexed by ambition, feverish for new gains,
Love just these gentler lives that gleam in calm
Below the fret and tumult of their own.
The gaunt crag somewhere throws its blot of shade,
And oft a pastoral meadow harbors it.
Yet do not dream, sweet girl, my love shall gloom
Thy future; glorious, rather, may it wrap
The destiny it fain would clasp and mould.

I am not one that tamely doth relax
His grip on power well-clutched in fingers firm.
Kiss me.

SYLVIA.

Thy kiss breeds terror yet delight.

BLONDIVAL.

Terror will fade from it ; delight, please fate,
Shall linger till we two stand crowned and throned.
Nay, do not start and tremble.   I am strong.
Deep is the tide I swim, and deeper yet
'Twill wax ere shallower ; yet I'll breast its rush
And bear thee with me in these buffeting arms !
                    (*The Queen enters, discovering them.*)

THE QUEEN.

Nay, wherefore let those arms untwine themselves?
Anguish hath lost its novelty of pang ;
Days ere to-day I knew thee what thou art.
                                        (*Exit Sylvia.*)
Poor girl ! I do not hate her, though I might.
Her sensitive spirit should not bruise its wings
Thus piteously in thy harsh copse of thorns.
Nor do I blame her ; 'twere as well to blame
The delicate bird-breast, not the shaft it sheathes.

BLONDIVAL.

His hand that led you where those draperies fall,
Was Malmondel's, who hath been my bitter foe
Since you, his cousin, wed me.

THE QUEEN.

Malmondel
Told nothing.   I had waited.   Eavesdropper
Neither I was nor would be, though folk said
One might but lift an eyelid to discern
Thee and thy paramour commingled thus.
No, Blondival, the spy that spied on thee
Was woman's misery, woman's hate of guile.
All is so different, now . .   I scarce can phrase
How wrath is dashed subservient unto grief.
This was your love—the love that bought a throne!

BLONDIVAL.

A three months' throne.   Fine recompense indeed!

THE QUEEN.

For what?   The proof that thou art grossly false?

BLONDIVAL.

You spoke of wrath.   Tempt not mine.   'Tis a king's.

THE QUEEN.

False, false . . immeasurably false ! You dare
Flaunt in my face this kingship I have wrought ?

BLONDIVAL.

Yes ; from the height thyself did build I dare
Look veto, autocracy.   Recall thine oath.

THE QUEEN.

Recall it ? Canst thou know the sacredness
It meant and means, O traitorous profligate ?

BLONDIVAL.

Come, since I am king at thy decree, forbear,
Lest I shall turn against thee thine own gift.

THE QUEEN.

There is no loathsome act of infamy
I should expect not now from thy base heart.
It is my shame that I should love thee still,
'Tis even a sort of horror to myself.
A girl, they taught me that no fault of man
Rated more meanly than ingratitude.
I did not dream that love could live at all
When scorn became its mate and counsellor.
Now do I see the terrible hardihood
Of love, which flowers in air grown taint and mirk.

BLONDIVAL (*in wrath*).

These two short royal months of mine have bred
Intolerance for such flame of rude revolt.
Bethink you, madam, that your palace-walls
Hold chambers where the axe may dint the block,
Live necks being cleft between them.   Did I choose,
I could this day do some such deed as those
Emperors of Rome's rich dying grandeurs did.
Half am I willed so through mere sight of thee,
In thy pale accusation and contempt.

THE QUEEN.

I see ; this power I gave hath made thee drunk.
Then, too, thou wouldst usurp the isle and set
Sylvia beside thee as new spouse.   For years
None dreamed how Nero hid that devil in him.
I dreamed it not of thee ; else had I shrunk
From squandering thus my kingdom.   Still, the oath
I swore thee stays inviolate.   More than this,
The imperishable love I bear thee yet
Makes me desire to probe in utmost way
Thy capability of dark unfaith.

BLONDIVAL.

Rightly thou sayst I am grown drunk with power.
Moreover, in harsh truth, I do avow

That every word of love my lips have breathed
Into thine ear was falsehood.   Void thy throne,
And leave me, with what statecraft I can wield,
To play upon thy people's whims and greeds.
Fare from the isle.   We have spoke of Rome.   Perhaps
'Twill grant, if deftly bribed, our clear divorce.
These are brute blows I am dealing ; such were
    best ;
I sicken of artifice ; the man I was
Henceforth shall sink beside me like a cloak
Tossed from the shoulders ; he that actually
I am shall flare defiant and shameless forth.

THE QUEEN.

Monster !   And I have loved thee, and still love !

BLONDIVAL.

Put then that stubborn love to test, and smooth
My path toward kingly permanence.

THE QUEEN.

Not so.
To loan my kingdom has been folly enough ;
I will not hurl it into ruin.   If death
Take me at thy decree, let Malmondel
Succeed me, avenge me, strike thee from thy prey.

He is the next heir.   May he rightlier reign
Than I have done !

BLONDIVAL.

     If he doth reign at all,
This Malmondel I hate as I hate thee !

THE QUEEN.

Thou canst not hate me, Blondival.   I stand
Between thyself and thy base-hungering hope ;
Thy sin stares large and hideous ; yet I say
It is not possible thou hatest me.

BLONDIVAL.

Some stealthy scheme lurks here to trap me tight.
Yet think not thou shalt win by devious wiles.
Never in all earth's annals hath it chanced
That mortal woman could prove meek as thou,
Save guile crouched tiger-wise below her looks.
And yet, whate'er the plot thou hatchest, know
My influence with the soldiery hath waxed
Already great ; I shall die hard, be sure.

THE QUEEN.

Thou shalt not need to die through choice of mine.

BLONDIVAL.

So then thou art loath to foil and raze me quite?

THE QUEEN.

Yes; but thou aimest to destroy thyself.

BLONDIVAL.

By heaven, I aim to do no such wild thing.
But thou wilt seek to thwart this lust I show
For individual empire?   Answer plain.

THE QUEEN.

The words that late I spoke unaltering bide.
Thou hast heard them.   Read their portent as thou
    choose.

BLONDIVAL.

Woman, what art thou?

THE QUEEN.

                        Once I was thy queen.
I am now thy conscience.   King, beware of me!

BLONDIVAL.

King!   'Tis a syllable that fires my soul!
I'll tell thee how I fear thy cautionings.
The guards are yonder.   See, I summon them.

                                        (*Guards enter.*)

This woman dies to-morrow.   Escort her hence.

THE QUEEN (*to guards, as they stand aghast*).

Your duty!   Dare you flout the King's command?

(*She goes out with the guards.*)

BLONDIVAL.

I shall not be the first who strove to grasp
A crown by wading through its wearer's blood.

III.

(*A prison-chamber in the palace. A headsman, beside
    block, with axe. The Queen appears, with
    guards. She signals to the headsman, who turns
    away.*)

THE QUEEN.

What?   You refuse obedience to your king?

(*She kneels before the block.*)

A GUARD.

Sure, 'tis some fearful jest, your majesty.

THE QUEEN (*still kneeling*).

The King hath ordered.   Bid the headsman act.

(*Loud murmurs are heard outside.*)

What sounds are those?

GUARD.

The people in angry throngs
Would break impetuous through the palace gates.
They have learned of danger threatening their loved
    Queen,
And rush—

THE QUEEN.

Quick, headsman! To thy darksome task!
Thou wilt not? Nay, 'tis treason if thou pause.
                (*Crashing noises. The Queen rises again.*)
The people are streaming through the courtyard, now?
They have burst the gates?

GUARD (*looking through window at back*).

'Tis true, your majesty.
And now Duke Blondival—

THE QUEEN.

You mean the King!

GUARD.

—Hath met them. He would fain command their heed.
His face is pale; his eyes dart fire. They note
His desperate bearing and before him troop.

He speaks of thee, our Queen.   He dares to say
That thou art dead from sudden malady,
That he will reign far worthier in thy place.   .   .

THE QUEEN.

What more   .   .   what more ?·

GUARD.

The people are wild with wrath.
They shout "assassin" from their myriad throats.
He towers engirt with soldiery, but these
Look doubtful in allegiance.   .   .   Now they join
The multitude, and fling their arms away.

THE QUEEN.

And he ?   And he ?

GUARD.

'Tis horrible past words !
Believing him thy murderer, they have torn
The Duke in pieces ; bloody and dripping, glare
His fragments ; never men so bore themselves
Like ravening beasts until this riot hour.

VOICES OUTSIDE.

Vengence ! Our dear dead Queen for vengeance calls !

GUARD.

Hark how they love thee! Shall I shout to them
That thou art saved?

THE QUEEN.

That I am saved? From what?

GUARD.

Why, death at that fiend's hands.

THE QUEEN (*drawing forth dagger*).

I loved that fiend!
Go, tell Prince Malmondel that he is King.

(*She falls dead.*)

THE TEARS OF TULLIA.

ROME shook with tyrannies. A bloated face,
 Vile for all vices that debase,
Glowered and menaced from the imperial place.

Men said " Caligula " below their breath,
 Shivering, as one that faintly saith
In some new deadlier way the old word " death."

That robe which once round Cæsar drooped sublime,
 Draggled and frayed, though not with time,
Flaunted from every fold wet stains of crime.

The empire of the world had fallen so low,
 Inertly it saw its own blood flow,
As treason's black brood dealt it many a blow

Deeper at each fresh ignominy it sank
 In mires of cowardice more rank,
Scourged by a monster and a mountebank.

Where vast the arena of the circus lay,
   Loosed lion or tiger, day by day,
Would flesh its fangs in shuddering human prey.

Throned o'er the slaughter sat with purple guise,
   With laureled brows, with wine-bleared eyes,
He whom to gaze upon was to despise.

Yet regnant thus, with crime for kith and kin,
   Did this crowned cut-throat seek to win
A hideous immortality out of sin.

His infamies caught splendor, like the fires
   That leapt in fury from those pyres
Where wives would watch their lords burn, sons their
      sires.

He seemed as one whose insolence erects
   A fane to his own dire defects,
With rapine, butchery, lust, for architects,—

A pile through haze of history to uprear,
   At every deed pure lives revere,
Its towering jibe, its monumental sneer! . .

And yet even he, Caligula, could feel
  Moods to his fiend-swayed soul appeal
Wherefrom the shadow of clemency would steal.

By some caprice no courtier could explain,
  He looked with favor, not disdain,
On Livius, a young noble of his train.

When weary of insult, lechery, murder, all
  Wherewith his madness held in thrall
Rome's cringing crowds, on Livius he would call.

From the massed purple cushions where he lay,
  " Read me some poet," he would say,
" My Livius, in your wise melodious way."

Then the youth, bowing with complaisance meek,
  In his rare lute-like tones would speak
Line after line from Homer's golden Greek.

And once, when kneeling at the tyrant's knee,
  Rapt by unwonted passion, he
Had read the dark wrongs of Andromache,

Caligula half-raised his drowsy head,
  And with the smile men quaked at, said :
" My Livius, thou hast eloquently read !

"None but a lover could so treat this theme ;
   And therefore thou, if rightly I deem,
Hast felt the full deep sorcery of love's dream.

"Would the kind gods had let me feel it, too !—
   The gods that guard me as they do ! . .
Nay, my sweet Livius, does report say true

"That thou hast loved, from boyhood sheer till now,
   Tullia, the maid with vestal brow,
Patrician Publius' grandchild, and dost vow

"Unflinching virtue, continence complete,
   Scorn of thy young blood's hardiest beat,
Till thou and she in marriage-bonds may meet?

"Nay, Livius, dost thou love this maid so well?
   I charge thee, in all fair frankness tell
How strong is thy subservience to her spell."

Then, smitten as by the pang that barbs a spear,
   Livius felt throes of mortal fear,
Not for himself, but one divinely dear.

He thought of how this royal vulture fed
   On multitudes of guiltless dead,
With beak that ever bode unsurfeited ;—

Of deeds that showed like some demoniac boy's
   Whom no malevolence gluts or cloys,
With rack, bowl, dagger and gibbet for their toys ;—

Of how Tiberius through his foul schemes died,
   Silanus had sought suicide,
And Orestilla had been stolen a bride

Even at the altar from her bridegroom's arms . .
   Remembering these and countless harms
Dastard as these, Livius with strange alarms

Thrilled as he murmured : " Emperor,. if the sky
   Made every star that hangs on high
A word of fire for me to answer by,

" Still vainly, in spite of such all-grasping speech,
   My love for Tullia could I teach—
Its force, its faith, its rapture and its reach ! "

So spake the youth, tumultuously.   A frown
   Dragged the prone despot's eyebrows down.
" Such love," he sneered, " my Livius, courts renown !

" What sayst thou if I seek a way to prove
   This vaunted value of thy love,
And how the ambition of its flame above

" Myriads of lesser lights doth dart and shine ?
  What sayst thou, favorite fool o' mine "
(Here a full snarl broke), " should my mood incline

" To test this love by some unique ordeal,
  And find if thou, who art sworn so leal,
Canst from the imaginary pluck the real,

" And prove to me, to all men, past a doubt,
  That adoration thus devout
Blindfold may trace its precious object out ? "

Pale turned young Livius, understanding not,
  Dreading some despicable plot,
While from the Emperor's lips bleak laughter shot,

Unpitying as when bared white bodies quailed
  While the lash bit—when stout hearts failed
While to the gaunt cross hands and feet were nailed !

" Go ! " cried Caligula. . . A moment more,
  And arms of strong slaves, by the score,
Had pushed poor Livius past the tyrant's door.

Alone they left him in a spacious hall,
  Brooding on what grim doom might fall,
What freak diabolic waited to appal,—

Till, at the close of one slow hour, he heard
   The bolts that held him captive stirred,
Obedient to Caligula's loud word.

Then with a smile where sly derision slept,
   The Emperor past the portal stept,
And straightway two strong minions lightly leapt

Toward Livius; o'er his eyes with speed they rolled
   A bandage of such envious fold
That by quick night all vision was controlled.

Quite still he stood, resisting not; he knew
   Resistance in a trice would hew
From mercy its last piteous residue.

" Fate, work your worst on me," his fleet thoughts ran;
   " Ere now full many a nobler man
Hath bowed below this arch-assassin's ban.

" So Tullia dies not with me, I shall bless
   Calamity for its kindliness,
And garner consolation from distress!"

But even as thus he mused, the air with sound
   Of numerous footfalls did abound,
Like plash of delicate rain on grassy ground,

And through the wide-flung doors, with timorous tread,
   With each a lovely and low-bent head
Half shadowing her bewilderments of dread,

Came twenty as bloomful maidens as the dome
   Of lucid heaven o'erarching Rome
Had ever beamed on.   Hence at speed from home

All had perforce been summoned by the sway
   Of him, unscrupulous to pay
Their lives in penalty for their delay.

Now rose the tyrant's voice, that seemed to kill
   The silence brutishly, such ill
Its every note was packed with, pealing shrill.

" Livius," its words came, " with a poet's tongue
   Hast thou belauded Tullia, young,
Radiant, thy love ; but here in beauty among

" A sisterhood of other beauteous mates,
   Thy recognition she awaits,
Thy swift intuitive welcome supplicates.

" Let now this boasted adoration dare
   Its magic energy declare ;
I bid thee touch on brow, cheek, eyelids, hair,

" Each maid of these assembled, till thou find
  The enslaving mistress of thy mind,
Being blind thyself as Love, thy god, is blind.

" Yet if by touch of hand upon her face
  Thou failest, braggart boy, to trace
Rightly her lineaments, not mere disgrace

" May wreak revenge on thy rash head, but she,
  Tullia, and thou, her choice, must be
Bound. each to other and cast within the sea !

" So shalt thou learn what ecstacies belong
  To love, with all its bonds made strong
As death's own lean clasp in the engirding thong.

" Yea, thou shalt learn of love that though it fly
  So lofty and in so large a sky,
Low may it sink at last, and darkly die ! ".   .   .

The looks of all save Livius now were turned
  On Tullia, whose amazed eyes burned
With agony,—then with adjuration yearned.

Scorn answered only from the Emperor's gaze ;
  Fierce to the grouped girls rang his phrase :
" One after one seek Livius, till he lays

"A hand upon your faces, dusk or fair,
  Searching for his lost Tullia there
In each! . . Obey me, or falter if ye dare!"

None dared to falter; slowly all drew near
  Livius, who stood with mien austere
That told what pain must make his veiled eyes drear.

Yet the hand shook not that erelong he laid
  On the first face of those arrayed
Before him, and with loitoring touch essayed

To prove alone by tactual sense what sight
  Would instantly have solved aright,
If given one vague ray of divulging light.

Still, eager and yet with impotence, he sought!
  Face after face, being swept thus, brought
But worse confusion to his laboring thought.

" I cannot find thee, Tullia ! " rose his cry,
  Freighted with torture. " We will die
Together, and curse the gods in our last sigh !"

And yet even here, while thick sweat damped his brow,
  A courage tyranny could not bow
Nerved him once more, and made him sweep forth,
    now,

For the last time to the last face his hand .   .
  Then suddenly, as by joy unmanned,
He shouted ;   " Pitying gods, I understand !

" These tears have told me !   Look, my hand is wet
  With their sweet testimony !   I set
My life and hers on the dear amulet

" Their tidings proffer !   *None has wept but she !*
  I have found thee, Tullia !   Love's decree
Can teach even blindness a new way to see !".   .   .

Before his final word impetuous rung,
  Poor Tullia with loud sobs had sprung
To clasp his neck—had wildly about it clung.

So cruelty had been slain by love ; and they
  Who saw Caligula that day,
Clothed in atrocity, were still wont to say

(Long after vengeful massacre had wrought
  End of his villainy, as it ought),
That just when Livius found the face he sought,

Learning glad Tullia by her tears to tell,—
  Tears also from the Emperor fell,
Strange tears, as if dawn's dews were seen in hell !

THE DYING ACTOR.

WHAT time is it? Seven o'clock, you say? Why,
    then, I should be at the theatre soon.
Ah, no. . . Lying here, day after day, has set my
    intellect out of tune.
I remember, now. . . It was weeks ago . .
    thank God I have savings left me still;
We actors were always given, you know, to die without
    paying the doctor's bill!

Nay, life has not blended, at the last, that bitter tor-
    ment with wasted health;
And yet, as I search the perished past, how I seem to
    have flung away my wealth!
'Twas easily gained, 'twas rashly spent, in times when
    my looks were a thing to laud,
When a bevy of fragrant notes were sent on the
    mornings after I played in *Claude!*

How the stubborn critics would wage their fight as to
    what had made me the people's choice!
Some swore it was merely my stately height, and a
    tricksy throb in my mellow voice.

Yet I thrilled my hearers and moved to tears, and I
    charmed them, whether they would or no ;
There were nights in those distant youthful years
    when the whole house rang to my *Romeo.*

But none could chide me for being proud while the
    fame I won was most broadly spread ;
Though the women's praises were always loud, it is
    certain they never turned my head.
I was stanch to my friends through worst and best ;
    that truth is my life's one spotless page ;
They have played their parts and gone home to rest ;
    I am talking here on an empty stage.

'Tis a sombre end for so bright a piece, this dull *fifth*
    act of the parting soul,
Ere the last sad *exit* has brought release, and the
    great green curtain begins to roll !
Yet though they have left me, those trusted friends, I
    cannot but fancy their absence means
That they wait outside till my own part ends, and will
    join me somewhere behind the scenes.

I see them here while I dream and doze . . There
    was Ralph, too reckless and wild by half,

With his ludicrous Punchinello nose and his full superb
    low-comedy laugh.
There was chubby Larry, with flaxen hair, who
    secretly longed to be dark and slight,
And believed his *Hamlet* a great affair, but was better
    in *Falstaff* any night.

There was lean grim Peter, so much in vogue, who
    could govern an audience by his wink ;
There was brilliant Hugh, with his witty brogue, his
    leaky purse and his love for drink ;
And then there was rosy old Robert, too, with whom
    bitter fortunes were hard at strife,
Who felt himself born a Macready, and who had been
    handing in letters all his life.

But more than these, there was brown-eyed Kate, true,
    generous, brave, and her own worst foe,
With a love no insults could alienate from the bad
    little husband who wronged her so.
Poor Kate ! She would call to her lovely face that
    radiant smile, in the nights long-fled,
And act *Lady Teazle* with dazzling grace while the
    heart in her bosom ached and bled !

There was ancient Clarissa, feeble, gray, who had kept
    to the last her queenly ease,
And held herself still in so grand a way as an English
    duchess or French marquise.
There was plump little Emily, hailed with roars, at the
    best in manners not over-nice,
But who counted her loyal slaves by scores, upstairs
    in the gloom of the paradise.

And one . . . Oh, Amy, I dare not own *your*
    love as a friend's love, weak of worth,
Though we swore the most sacred promise known, and
    were bound by the strongest bond on earth!
Ah me! at the summons of death's weird spell, I can
    see you, while pangs of memory start,
In the waiting-maid rôles you did so well, pirouetting
    with sweet unconscious art!

I remember the play when first we met—how your
    glad eyes haunted me from afar,
As you tripped and prattled, a pert soubrette, while I
    was a grave majestic " star."
I remember when wedded joys were new . . the
    dawn of the troubles, the scandals coarse . .
The last mad passionate interview . . the wrangle
    of lawyers ; the stern divorce !

With wrathful scorn I have cursed your name ; yet if
truth be said, as I here avow,
We were both to blame, we were both to blame ; in
my soul I know it and feel it now !
A new strange light seems to break and shine on that
dreary story of woful shame ;
If the sin was yours it was also mine ; we were both
to blame—we were both to blame !

* * * * * *

Those dear lost friends, they have grouped afresh in
the green room, quite as they used to do ;
And Ralph has been laughing at Larry's flesh, and
Peter is growling a joke to Hugh,
And Robert complains of his lowly lot, and Emily gos-
sips with Kate. . . Ah, well,
You may all be shadows, but *I* am not, while I listen
here for the Prompter's bell !

VICISSITUDE.

ONE must allow (although within these walls
    It be discourtesy to air the fact)
Our good Mæcenas mixes, at his balls,
    With something more of energy than tact.

To-night the company both charms and bores :
    A few choice souls, as rare as perfect pearls ;
Toadies by dozens ; humbugs by the scores ;
    Ladies with " views," in spectacles and curls.

A multicolored masquerade of mind,
    Whose masques are seldom dropped, as slight heed
        tells,
And in whose costumes multiplex we find
    A marked preponderance of caps-and-bells.

'Twould be no matter for extreme surprise
    To meet the new pet poet here to-night.
Ah, see him—that pale stripling with large eyes,
    Beset by lion-hunters, left and right.

A forceful face, though showing, you might say,
   Too proud a smile, a triumph too elate.
Why, the boy needed bread but yesterday,
   And lo, to-day he breaks it with the great !

Speaking of poets . . *apropos* . . I am
   Still slow to see for what cause, subtly fine,
The critics once applauded and now damn
   That shabby man with white hair, taking wine.

TWO SCENES
IN THE LIFE OF BEAU BRUMMELL.

I.

1810.

(Brummell's dressing-room, in Chapel Street, London. He is standing before a mirror. Lord Alvanley has just entered, ushered in by Pierre, the valet.)

BRUMMELL.

It's you, Alvanley? 'Gad, you're punctual, sir !
Pardon, my lord, but is it quite good taste
To show such damnable exactitude
In keeping one's appointments ? . . Pierre, you
    dog,
Take these piled coats and waistcoats from the couch
Their villanous tailoring cumbers, that my lord
May sit a moment till my toilet's done.
'Faith, Heaven's a place, in my theology,
Where every tailor that cuts badly here
Finds himself badly cut on entering there. . .
Excuse me if I don't shake hands, my lord ;
The tying of this cravat-- my tenth to-night—
Trembles. I think, on coy perfection's verge. . .

Ah! one more turn o' the wrist . . I have it!
    Look!
Answer, Alvanley, as you love true speech:
Was ever neckerchief more eloquent
In silent praise of its creator?—Pierre,
How's this, you unctuous knave? A speck of dirt
Fouling my coat-sleeve? Zounds, I'd like to be
Sultan or caliph for as long a space
As it would take to see you bow-strung, sirrah!
Alas, Alvanley, these are piteous times
When suffering masters cannot strangle rogues
Like Pierre, without they call it murder! (Stop
Grinning, you dolt, and fetch my cane and gloves!)
There, now, Alvanley, see the style of man
You might have been if fortune had bestowed
Her favers equally on both of us!
Still, why should you or anyone repine?
Alvanleys are not common, I'll admit,
But the real Brummell comes not oftener
Than once a century. Nature saves herself
For these imperial efforts to produce
An unexceptionable gentleman!
Art does the rest, and kindly pedestals
The statue, frames the picture.

                          (*Offers snuff-box.*)

                              Neat, my lord?
A gift from our fat friend, the Regent.   He
Slipped it within my hand, the other night,
At supper—rather vulgarly, I thought;
But I forgave his condescension, since
The silverwork's Venetian and most rare.
Besides, poor fellow, he was ripely drunk
On his own odious claret. Fox was there,
Pretentious, wordy, talking one to death ;
And poor Dick Sheridan, that Grub Street wag
Whom George *will* tolerate, read verse on verse
Of pointless fustian, till I ceased to count
My yawns—their number scaled the infinite !
I lost a hundred guineas afterward
At Watier's, closing thus a dreary night
Of memorable boredom, and awoke
Next morning with this royal gift to lay
Balm on my spleen.   'Twas filled with that vile snuff
The Prince takes; I replenished it, of course,
With something less barbaric, as you'll note.   .   .
Well, now, the Duchess claims us at her ball ;
I'd rather play at White's than go to her.
But then these Yorks are sensitive ; Her Grace
Thinks, too, a ball no ball not led by me.
I met the Duke in Bond Street yesterday ;

He took my arm, in his familiar style
(A style I don't approve of, yet endure),
And begged profusely I'd not disappoint.
Bah! how he smelt of brandy—and the hour
Scarce three o'clock! "Brummell, good friend," he
    urged,
" Deny it as they may, none shines like you
The star of London fashion!" . . I confess,
Alvanley, that this bungling compliment
Disgusted me so sharply I let fall
The Duke's arm, feigning I'd a twinge of gout
In mine . . . "Deny it as they may," forsooth!
Pray, *who* denies it? Who, indeed, I ask?
Some countrified old dowager, with four
Unmarriageably freckled girls? Or some
Finsbury tradesman, with more brass than sense,
Who fancied I would see him in the Park
Because at one o' the clubs, when play ran high
And hours were small, I borrowed graciously
A five-pound note? . . . Detractors, these, my
    lord!
Great personages cast great shadows. Fools
Never so loudly prate as when their theme
Trenches upon their betters. Who to-night
Will get so glad and warm a smile as I

From our magnificent Duchess? You shall mark!
Why, the whole company stands tip-toe now,
Waiting my entrance. We are early yet.
What say you if I let Pierre uncork
A bottle of my prime Burgundy—a gift
From Beaufort—smooth as velvet? . . You'll be
    late?
Why, then, Alvanley, you'll be late *with me*—
Which means, the Duchess will forgive us both. . .
You hear, Pierre, you rascal? Serve us, quick!

II.

1836.

(*A shabby room in the Hotel d'Angleterre, Caen, France.
    Beau Brummell, decrepit and haggard, stands clad
    in an old, faded dressing-gown, near a table lit
    with one sputtering tallow candle. A man who
    serves him for the sake of charity, has just
    appeared.*)

BRUMMELL.

So, François —— Pierre —— no, François—here at
    last?
I've waited you a small eternity.
What's o'clock. Nine? Why, then we should begin

Our entertainment. . . Come, man—come! Don't
    stand
Staring like such a dullard . . Who's first guest?

FRANÇOIS (*mechanically*).

His Grace of Devonshire . . Ah, no! *Her* Grace,
The Duchess. (*Il me gêne, ce vieux galant!*)

(*No one enters.*)

BRUMMELL (*with his old famous bow*).

Duchess, believe me, I am overwhelmed!
How exquisitely good of you! . . Not there!
Nay, I forbid that you shall sit save here,
In this, the especial chair reserved for you.
Dear Lady Hester Stanhope broidered it
With her fair hands,—but not so fair by half
As yours . . The Duke comes with you? . .
    Ah, dear Duke,
What artful service have you done grim time
That he rewards you with such hey-dey youth?

FRANÇOIS.

My Lord Alvanley.

BRUMMELL.

I am charmed, my lord!

FRANÇOIS.

The Earl of Westmoreland . .   Lord Delamere.

BRUMMELL.

This equals Almack's on a gala night!

FRANÇOIS.

The Lady Stormont and Sir Watkyn Wynne.

BRUMMELL.

Europe's no happier man than Brummell . .   Nay,
He'll throw in all the other continents!
For here are both their Royal Highnesses
Of York, to make my gathering past compare!
Now, ladies, gentlemen, your host implores
That for a few sweet jovial hours you'll cast
Remembrance of your rank and privilege
Clear to the breezes of to-morrow's dawn.
I've cards and dice ; I've wine and edibles ;
I've all resource wherewith to make it seem
Other than strange the loftiest in our land
Should deign acceptance from the lowliest there. . .
Alvanley smiles ; he has heard me speak so oft
In different strain.   But then a gentleman
Should never be so grand a hypocrite
As when he is a gentleman at home !

You laugh   .   .   and how your laughter rings ! Well,
    well,
Laugh and be merry   .   .   I—
        (*His demeanor changes ; he sinks into arm-chair.*)
                Pageant made of ghosts,
How swift you vanish with my altering mood !
O, Brummell, bald and toothless maunderer,
Juggler with shadows, driveller, harlequin
Tumbling in tattered motley !   Once I reigned
A kind of king among that spectral throng !—
A king, but with how brittle and brief a crown !
Ah, me ! if those dead years of mine could raise
A million taunting voices, each would cry
"Fool" at me in my ruin and shame this hour !
And they whose favoring smiles were vital warmth
To my poor gorgeous and ephemeral day—
What cared they if I throve or lamely fell ?
They had their pedigrees, their rent-rolls, their
Clarion patrician names, their palaces
In Surrey or Kent or Warwickshire, their droves
Of servants,—and their dainty *ennui*, that sought
Diversion from the first apt mountebank
Whose trickeries could allure its light caprice.
They watched me strut and preen my plumes a while,
Fostered my peacock arrogance, beset

With ironies of flattery my least whim,
And then—why, then came Calais, flight from debt,
Exile, awakening after giddy dream,
Struggle, dependence, pity as pitiless
As though 'twere scorn a school-boy had spelt ill,
And last, this penury, with frail health to lend
Its tooth a hardier venom. . .   So the tale
Of Brummell's glory is ended ! . .   And I knew,
I knew when my most dazzling tinsels blazed,
That life at worthiest might have meant for me
Love, peace, joy, home, immeasurably far
From all that fever, mockery and pretense ! . .
Ah, well ! 'tis given most men with souls and brains
To let the boats they sail in strike bleak rocks
Or steer them by the undeceptive stars ! . .
I chose my own mad pilotage, and now
Whom dare I blame but self for wreck like this ?

(His head droops very low.)

FRANÇOIS (touching his shoulder).

Pardon, monsieur . .   I think your *fête* is done .
The dukes and duchesses are all *partis ;*
'Tis time monsieur should sleep.

BRUMMELL (lifting head).

I wish it were !

Feb., 1887.

THARAK AND THE LION.

NEAR a wide Asian desert, ruled of old
King Thalmak, monarch of a Median race.
Foes oft had gloomed his realm with ire and threat,
Though past a decade peace had reigned therein,
Bought at the gory price of countless lives.
For Thalmak towered a warrior vast of shape,
With breasts where sinews bulged like knotted ropes
And wrists whose veins were large as common thews.
Down o'er his fierce brows poured the tangled curls ;
His hands were hammer and broadsword both in one ;
He had slain a hundred men in equal fight ;
To meet his eyes when wrathful was to see
Globed lightning—and to die of it, perchance.
Yet many a mood of clemency was his ;
The people he swayed were loyalty's firm self,
Knowing him just in council, shrewd in pacts,
And roughly leal to those he roughly loved.

One son had Thalmak, now at manhood's verge,
Named Tharak, stately of shape as any palm
Whose green crest peers to see the Caspian flash

Beyond lone stretches of Cadusian slopes.
Yet though in brawn and stature sire and boy
Were like as are two bosks of terebinth
Pluming high Zagros, yet the younger lacked
All hint of savagery in face and mien.
So mild he loomed, with blue deep thoughtful gaze
And lips the ceaseless ambush of a smile,
That many a watcher mused concerning him—
" It is no wonder they so oft have said
His mother was the daughter of a star."

For so the tale in earlier years had run.   .   .
King Thalmak, while his throne was girt with hates,
Passed home, one twilight, through a land of hills,
Victorious after terrible clash of spears
With his own brother's host, the desperate hordes
Of Parmys.   Tired, he paused to pitch his tents
Beside a stream that brawled through tamarisks.
The army on shield and sword slept all night long,
And Thalmak, after parley among his peers,
Flung himself in full harness on a couch
The slaves had fashioned from stray wools and silks.
But when with reverences they passed from him
And every noise except the hurrying stream
Was hushed, King Thalmak, it is chronicled,

Rose, tingling from a dream of that dread sort
Which jars the nerves of soldiers after fray,
Ere yet the first light sleep hath merged itself
Into such opiate blank as mends fatigue.
" Oh, peace," he murmured, " I that oft craved war,
Desire thee now! I am sick at last of fight!
Visit me, peace, Amaiti, by the will
Of thy great lord and mine, the worshipful
Ahuramazda!" Therewith, speaking so,
He cleft the curtains of his tent and moved
Out where in opulence of pallor swarmed
The brooding stars. His army in apathy
Lay prone like swaths of new-shorn wheat ; the winds
Had shod themselves with sandals echoless
And to mysterious whispers tuned their throats.
" O peace," again he murmured, " visit me ! "
Then suddenly, as though in sweet response
The oracular night had heard and heeded him,
He looked upon a woman, white of robe,
With eyes where chastity and passion met,
And brow so pure and so self-luminous
It seemed to make a moonlight of her face.

When on the morrow in triumph he drew near
His capital, between the palace-gates

A veiled shape entered swiftly at his side.
But none had seen his new mysterious mate
Save in this fleet phantasmal way; for weeks
The court with gossip and conjecture burned.
Who was the stranger?   Whence her race and name?
How had she fallen upon the King?   Where now
Did she stay hid among the multiplex
Chambers of his close-barred seraglios?   .   .   .
Meanwhile the King himself was taciturn
As his own trusted mutes, yet from his mien
A secret joy would flash its mellow ray
And many a phrase or gesture now was clad
With clemency where likelier in the past
Had been curt dealing.   So a year wore out
And all this while 'twas rumored that aloof,
In rooms one tiger-lily of luxury,
Bode the pent lady, and that a subtle fear
Clouded the King's deep love, lest possibly
Those delicate symmetries that lured him so
Might fade as fades a fern at hint of frost ;
Since not with waste of malady she drooped,
And yet the change to slenderer, airier,
Kept ever growing.   And when that year had fled,
Still was it rumored that her shape at last
Glimmered as immaterial as a ghost's,

Though gifted with such charm of willowy curves
A man would die to clasp it, while her eyes
Held all fate's gloom below each ivory lid,
Yet with warm Orient langours ever brimmed.
And Thalmak, seeing her piteously wane,
Trembled with anguish, for he guessed or knew
That she was born of that bright sisterhood
Called Children of the Stars, who had come down
To earth among the Scythians, wedding them,
Being spirits made like women out of light.
And one day in his passionate clasp, 'twas told,
Her frame to vaporous nullity dissolved,
Even as the pangs of childbirth racked her sore ;
And while intangibly a wreath of haze,
Globed with two dark similitudes of eyes,
Floated above the unhappy King, he heard
That frighted wail which leaves a new-born child.

For hours he longed in frenzy that the child
Might die, nor looked upon it, loathing it.
Then, as he lay and thrashed his couch of skins,
Or ploughed his riotous locks with rugged hand
While quivering mouth and nostril dumbly said :
" Would Heaven this grief, so gruesome in its qualms,
Were some live enemy I might front and kill,"

A trusted eunuch dared to bring the child
And kneel before him, holding it aloft.
"See, O my King," the eunuch still dared urge,
"How beauteous is the babe thy lost love bore!"

Then Thalmak, rising, sprang to seize his sword;
And would have slain the eunuch, but that here
A glance involuntary acquainted him
How beauteous was indeed the sleeping babe.
He paused, and from his clenched hand fell the blade
As falls a sapling by the abusive east
Flung prone; his great frame tremulous, he bent
And touched with awe the rose-tinge infantile
Of the small slumberer's cheek; impetuous tears
Gushed from his warrior gaze that had not flinched
When flying javelins wove their giddy nets
Below the steadfast sun, and zigzag fight
Bannered with shameless crimson the meek sward.

Not many days thereafter stood the King
Conspicuous on his palace porch, while throngs
Massed eagerly below him. From his crown
Ten flawless emeralds out of Petra blazed.
Near by, an Ethiop slave, on fire with gems,
Lifted the young child, Tharak, in a robe
Of silvery tissues like spun beams of stars.

Then the King took the child betwixt his hands
And showed it to the people, saying " I name
This boy mine heir, to reign when I am dust.
No other child begot of me shall reign
While he or any of his own line lives on.
This I decree, and by Ardibehest,
The spirit of truth, and Indra, god of war,
Charge ye to reverence him as future king."

Then all vowed fealty to young Tharak, save
A few that fled the realm and hid themselves,
Headed by Parmys, the King's brother, where
Great cliffs and delving gorges clogged the North.
For Parmys, pierced by envy and discontent,
Cried that this Tharak was in bastardy
Engendered, and that if no lawful heir
Issued from Thalmak's loins, himself must reign
When death made void the throne.   He subtly saw
That Thalmak looked upon no woman now,
And therefore counted that this treasured boy
Should bide the single barrier, as years lapsed,
Between his own ambitions and the hope
Of suzerainty.   Right he had counted : still,
The King, grown furious at his flight and spleen,
Arrayed against him droves of venturous troops

That pushed him from his fastnesses and faced
The auxiliaries he had lured or bought,
Shattering and scattering them by myriads.
But Parmys, like a stag in those wild steeps,
Hurried with safety from his wiliest foes
And gained a Scythian kinsman, a rude lord
Who hated Thalmak for some petty grudge,
As mean souls hate their betters. There these
    twain
Crouched vigilant of their chance, while more years
    rolled,
And Thalmak lived at peace with all the world.

Yet spite of tranquil times throughout his realm,
The King knew Parmys of that serpent sort
Which wraps malignancy in sloth and stealth.
He felt his own strength fail him ; sly disease
Crept through his veins with morbid indolence,
Warning yet weakening ; his court-doctors tried
In vain their drugs and simples, used in vain   •
Their spells of alchemy and exorcism.
He wasted as an oak whose day has waned,
Still with live gloss of greenery burgeoning,
Yet now no more that bounteous dome of shade
Where once hath loitered many a lyric breeze.

"Mine hour draws nigh," he thought, "and when it
    falls
I would my kingdom were to hardier hands
Entrusted.   Not that Tharak is below
Myself in valor and fortitude, for none
More martially than he doth sit his steed,
And none joys more at perils of the chase
While boar-tusks plunge, or tiger-mouths gape death.
And yet my Tharak hath not mettle in him
That makes a ruler.   Ever beats his heart
The enemy of his judgment.   For a twinge
Of pity, a throe of transient sympathy,
Quick would he toss his regal state aside
And with inferiors droop to comradeship.
Last month by some lorn tale a mere street-waif
So moved him that he plied the oaf with boons
And housed him like a satrap.   One week since,
He begged me spare a murderess, black with crime,
Because she had slain her sleeping paramour
In a mad fit of jealousy, and had leaned
Her lips to his while death was fluttering them,
And twined his hair with roses! . . Pah! the boy
Should learn that justice hath a dignity
Even kings must worship, and no crown will stick
So tight on even the most imperial head

But if its wearer bow himself too low
There be not risk the greedy dust will rise
To claim it! . . But how teach him these wise
    ways
Of rulership?   He is all complaisance, all
Deference and filial fondness—yet, ah me !
Better he burned with rebel insolence
Than let stray freaks of ruth so snare his mood !"

But while this very day the king thus mused,
A noble of rank and privilege drew nigh
And gave him tidings of the Prince, that shocked
For sheer disrelish.   Tharak and his train
Were hunting, five days gone, on that bleak land
Which verged the desert's treeless monotone,
When full in view a lion of splendid front
Broke from beyond a towering cone of sand.
The spear of every horseman poised its point,
But moveless in recumbent majesty
Staid the grand beast, nor proffered hint of flight.
Then someone said " He is sick ; his eyes are filmed,"
And soon another, " Oh, look, his paws are gashed
As if by conflict with a brother-brute !"
" Slay him at once !" a third cried, " or perchance
He may leap furious from his lassitude !"

But there the Prince, with gesture of command,
Silenced all parley, and in a moment more
Pressed his horse clear to where the lion crouched.
Shuddering, his watchers waited his fleet death ;
But, no ; the lion, in place of onslaught, reared
His tawny lips and roared voluminously
A vast funereal welcome.   Then the Prince,
Quitting his horse with one light spring, approached
Yet nearer, while his ghastly jeopardy
Made them that gazed upon him quake and sweat.
And he who told King Thalmak ended thus :
" O sire, no sooner was this wondrous deed
Of boldness wrought, to our surpassing awe,
Than straightway did the hurt beast thrust his tongue
Out toward the Prince's hand that fearless met
Such hideous courtesy ; and like a hound
Grateful for heed, we saw the monster lick
That palm which one day (please the gods, yet far !)
Shall grasp thy sceptre.   Turning with a smile,
The Prince enjoined on us we should bring forth
What oils and lenitives the slaves had borne
To ease our own sore bruises got in hunt.
By Indra, sire, but such command seemed weird !
Still, we obeyed ; and tenderly thy son
Did wash and bind his new friend's gaping cuts ;

Nay, with the lion abode, and sent one half
His train (whereof I am parcel) cityward.
Yet ere we went it was his will to speak,
Erect, with hand that strayed amid the fleece
Of that dense yellow fell whereunder shrank
Great smoldering eyes, black-ringed, that seemed to
    dart,
Even in their dimness, rays of massacre.

"' Courtiers and friends,' he said, with the large voice
He hath from thee, the voice that holds a tone
Melodious as notes tolled by bells of gold,
' I choose to save, not slay, this couchant bulk.
For though the chase be glorious in its test
Of nerve, skill, courage, oft I have had my doubts
If we should thus on lives below us push
Contention shorn of every finer aim
Save such as fosters crude belligerence.   .   .
Nay, I have dreamed far suns may shine on days
When man shall hold it infamy to make
Of man his adversary, and all earth's feuds
Harmoniously shall meet in brotherhood !
But that is dream, dream only, and let it pass.   .   .
Here is no dream, this broken and bleeding shape
Our spears and bows had found so tangible

Except for these rough ills that maim his brawn.
Why, friends, if once we pluck from out our souls
All pity, it is forthwith as though we reft
Some garden of all blooms whence odors float.
Thrift, color, beauty of petal still remain,
But fragrance hath eternally retired.
Were we to kill this lion, it were to kill
The loftier something in our secret selves
That makes us more than he.   So let him live !' "

King Thalmak, hearing this quaint history, sighed,
And when, days afterward, the Prince returned,
Brown from long rural tarriance, he was fain
To chide the youth with splenetic reproach.
But soon came drifting into Tharak's eyes
That likeness of his dear dead mother's look
Which meant pain, memory, comfort intermixed,
And like a flash the father's heart grew soft.   .   .
"Where hast thou left thy lion, O laggard boy ?"
He said, with slow smile flickering through his
      beard.   .   .
And Tharak with responsive smile broke out :
" Has the tale reached thee, then ?" and flung himself
On the King's couch and clasped the royal feet,
Telling the tale once more with phrase that flowed

Oblivious of its own rich eloquence.
"Oh, father," he ended, "when I left my charge
He stood nigh whole in hardihood sublime.
I gave him back to the great desert sweeps,
I gave him back to liberty and power,
To murmurs that the earth-god, Mithra, makes,
To large discourses of the wind, Vayu.
I gave him back, nor grudged him all I gave,
Child of the solitude and monarch there,
With eyes that blink not at the torrid suns,
And limbs whose fleetness mocks the gray simooms.
For he is kinglier than we human kings;
He acts out all his nature, free from stint.
His very greeds are generous; what he takes
Of territory is but to loll upon
In transient rest, and his worst fights are waged
At the bluff dictates of his naked self,
Not cultured by ambition's wiles and crafts."

King Thalmak looked a long look on his son
Ere answering, and then only these few words
Fell from his lips, as though phrased half in dream:
" The gods befriend thee, my philosopher,
When thou shalt mount this throne I soon must
    quit!"

"Not soon!" cried Tharak. "Many a year shall pass
Ere the cold blight that orphans me shall curse
Thy realm with still more piteous orphanage!"

But Tharak's love spake no true prophecy;
For soon the King's distemper grievous grew,
And one fair night, while he lay calm and pale,
And the Prince watched beside him, he desired
That from a casement near his couch be drawn
Its draperies, letting beam full on his bed
The tacit stars. This done, he seemed at peace,
And stared long on the glistening dark as though
Its depths were drink, his own sight eager thirst.
Then twice or thrice low-whispering "She is there,"
He sought the sleep none lives that may elude.

Scarce were the pomps of burial consummate
When Parmys, from his watch-towers of North hills,
Came with an army of wild-eyed skin-clad men
To assault the city gates. But him with troops
Gathered in hot haste though redoubtable,
Tharak undaunted met. Nor would he brook
Siege for a single day, but crying "Attack,"
Unclamped the gates and past their threshold sent
A catapult of thick-serried men that split

His uncle's host in twain as 'twere a fowl
Cleft by the scullion who quick serves a feast.
But rallying both at left and right, the foe
Shot back with twofold shock, one mass being led
By Parmys, by his barbarous kinsman one.
For three long shuddering hours the fields were
     drenched
With death, and all the insulted blue above
Clamored with shrieks of pain.   Like mastiffs clutched
By famine fought the Scythians, and so near
Strove against Tharak's forces that their skill
As warriors failed of profit, and they flung
Spear or bow earthward, with drawn cutlasses
Gashing the Northmen's throats, like bulls' for girth.

But rout and ruin at last beset the son
Of Thalmak, though he fought, those three mad hours,
With such grand heat that round him where he fought
Bodies lay ramparted like upthrown earth.
For Parmys, while he panted from fatigue,
Rushed at him, and with treacherous underblow
Struck from his folded fists the sanguine sword
They leaned on.   Staggering, Tharak fell to earth,
Whereat five Scythians leapt upon his frame,
Disarming it and capturing him alive.

Like wind the news of Tharak's overthrow
Sped through his army, and in its wake dismay
Talked with despair. Triumphant, unopposed,
Parmys and all his followers passed erelong
Within the city. On every side they saw
Women, old men and children, terror-struck,
Expecting when the conqueror's hand should smite.
But Parmys aimed at no coarse tyrannies
Of subjugation. Subtle he was, not less
Than savage, and well knew his coming reign
Must plant the bastions of its permanence
In tricks of diplomatic artifice.
Wherefore, on that same day, when fears were
    lulled,
He spake before the assembled populace.

" Ye are my subjects," hailed he from the stairs
Of the wide palace-portico. " Our gods,
That equally are mine and yours, decree
My empery. Tharak, born a bastard prince,
Hath fallen below my just revolt. Yet now,
Because I know ye doubt if I shall rule
With such wise tact as fits a lawful king,
Learn from my lips, in solemn plight of faith,
How I shall wear my dear dead brother's crown

As though 'twere some live thing whose gems and
    gold
Could breathe me counsels caught from those large
    brows
That late have borne it.   Justice, mercy and love
Shall meet as ministers about my throne,
And war crouch only at my low footstool, kept
Like a leashed bloodhound from whose pinioned
    throat
Brave guardianship of country slips the bond."

Pausing, shrewd Parmys marked the multitude
Below him.   Quick the insidious words he phrased
Had wrought their calming consequence.   Yet cries
Rang soon from many an auditor :   "Our Prince ! "
" Tharak, or bastard or legitimate,
What fate shalt thou apportion him ? "   .   .   " Yes,
    tell
If death or exile be our Tharak's doom ! "

While so the tide of clamorous question surged,
Parmys, with looks that counterfeited well
Regret and pity, again found reachful voice :

" If there be those that deem the gods would help
This youth a wandering harlot hath begot,

I shall not shirk the test that either proves
He is prince, or verifies his base-born rank.
For, listen, it is but lately learned of me
That to the south gate of the city a band
Of hunters, all being ignorant if raged
Northward the fight I conquered in, have brought
A living lion, assailed by strategy
And captured thus, intent on proferring him
To Tharak, trophy and tribute both in one.
Therefore to-morrow, I do ordain, this beast
Caged in the public square shall front ye all,
And Tharak shall behind its bars be thrust.
Then, if no harm befall him where he bides,
I swear to vanish with my soldiery
From out the city and leave him once more King.
But if the lion assault him and so slay,
Then shall the message of the gods read clear
To every sense ; for surely it would not tax
Omnipotence like theirs to shield and save,
And surely I could not unto holier hands
Confide this cause, deep-freighted with such pith
Of import and so near the nation's weal."

Thus urged the wily conqueror ; and he laughed
Low in his own heart, packed with fell intrigue,

To note some faces of his listeners prove
That trust in Tharak's victory had sprung forth
From even so dismal an arbitrament.
For Parmys long ere now had coldly scoffed
At intercessions betwixt gods and men.
"They are heedless of us," he would jeer, "as we
Are heedless of the autumnal leaf that whirls."
And now in mockery to his bloody mates,
"I pave," he said, "my path toward facile sway.
They saw him worsted of our spears, but brim
With faith he is yet a demigod.   Full soon,
When he shall be devoured in sight of them,
This idiot cult of theirs will veer like wind."

That night the city slept, or seemed to sleep,
While even its very babes were sentinelled.
Many that loved their King (who loved him not
Of them that war had spared to hate his foes?)
Went whispering each with each: "The gods are
      cold ;
They love their loves and sin their sins aloof,
Oblivious of our frail mortality ;
This Parmys knows them in their dumb blind scorn."

But on the morrow, amid an eager throng,
The lion, incarcerate within its cage,

Glared from black bars.   Here willingly was led
Tharak ; who, pausing ere he neared his fate,
With sovereignty of gesture that forbade
The guards to harry or thwart his wish, remained
Moveless, and from his lips these words outflowed :

" My people, I bow to what our gods ordain.
Bow also ye.   If death lay hold on me,
Strive that your best obedience wed itself
To your best knowledge of desert in him
Wielding the sceptre.   Stifle, I charge of ye,
All hate for one that peradventure seeks
The goal which justice, to his own belief,
Makes duty, and bear in mind how motive lurks
Alike the cause and gauge of human sin.
So, ere ye name him tyrant, watch him well,
Being rather mindful of what good shall hap
Our state hereafter than what ill he wrought
On me, among the irrevocable dead.
For if he is confident my claim of rule
Be empty and valueless, perchance he finds
In my slain corpse a healthier civic boon
Than any a life of banishment might bring :
Since, were I far in exile, faction's mouth
Might ever snarl my name rebelliously,

And sow the realm with internecine feuds
Worse than war's candors when thy hotliest flare.
So now, farewell.   I have reigned a little space,
Yet in such reign have sought to serve high creeds.
Think not too tenderly of this my death,
For sorrow is foe of patience, and ye need
Stout hearts to bear these bodeful storms of change."

Thus having said, King Tharak turned and walked
Unfaltering to the cage, with his own hand
Set in its massive lock the massive key,
Oped wide the door, then closed it, and stood firm
Before the bristling and infuriate brute
That sprang to meet him.

              Many an eye was bathed
In tears.   Friends, foes, by equal thrills were moved,
Hearing his language of sweet tolerance,
Marking in brow, form, posture, his brave calm.

But as the lion approached him, lo, a smile
Bloomed bright from Tharak's lips !   He reached one
      hand
Serenely forth and stroked the creature's mane,
Knowing the sick beast he had soothed of yore.
And while its poignant eyes grew soft, he felt

The gods indeed had spoken! A mighty cry
Shot from the multitude as all now saw
The lion at Tharak's feet in meekness fawn,
Like some fond dog that greets a master's face
When tedious hours of absence bring him home.

Parmys grew livid, then, with wrath and fear,
Below the silk pavilion where he sat.
"A trick," he roared, " a lying and cheating trick!
Some sorcerer's impish work! Let both be slain!
Have at them, trusted Scythians, with your spears!"

But no man stirred, of all the enormous host;
As well might Parmys to deaf rocks have shrieked.
And seeing at last how Tharak from the cage
Came forth, and how the lion, at his light beck,
Followed him, with hard haste the false King leapt
To earth, and snatching from a warrior's hold
His long spear, darted for the arena where
Unarmed stood Tharak.

       Ill had Parmys planned,
If counting on the lion as always mild.
For while with spear uplifted he bore down
On Tharak, suddenly flamed the topaz eyes,
The amber body in one great bound shot out,

And torn to ghastly shreds the usurper lay,
A bleeding mockery of the man he was.

Thus Tharak to his rightful throne returned ;
For all the foe withdrew ere night had come,
Awed by what seemed miraculous evidence
That the gods' anger had flung Parmys low.

And Tharak, having led the lion again
Within its cage, decreed it should be borne
Back to the desert and there given once more
Its freedom. .   .   But when tales were told to him
Of how this lion had been a god disguised,
He mused and answered with a meaning smile :
" Yes, there is godliness in gratitude
Which makes even beasts that show it seem divine ! "

INTERMEZZO.

I.—THE WOOD-TURTLE.

GIRT with the grove's aerial sigh,
  In clumsy stupor deaf as fate,
Near this coiled naked root you lie,
  Impervious and inanimate !

Between these woodlands where we met,
  And your grim langour void of grace,
My glance, dumb sylvan anchoret,
  Mysterious kinsmanship can trace ;

For in your chequered shape are shown
  The miry black of swamp and bog,
The tawny brown of lichened stone,
  The inertness of the tumbled log.

But when you break this lifeless pause,
  And from your parted shell outspread
A rude array of lumbering claws,
  A length of lean dark snaky head,

I watch from sluggish torpor start
   These vital signs uncouth and strange,
And mutely murmur to my heart :—
   "Ah, me ! how lovelier were the change

" If yonder tough oak, seamed with scars,
   Could give some white wild form release,
With eyes amid whose wistful stars
   Burned memories of immortal Greece ! "

II.

ABOVE the porch, full in dawn's rosy view,
   Fringes of icicles hang glittering keen,
Traced clear against the pale heaven's crystal blue
   In splintry and vivid sheen.

And as their silver lances glassily clash
   With golden lances by the new day borne,
Through the sharp air unmelted they now flash
   A silent arctic scorn.

But while the grand sun mounts in dazzling state,
  My thoughts from these bleak snowy scenes have
      turned
To sultry and luxurious climes where late
  Noon's yellow fervors burned !

Still from the porch the icicles gleam chill ;
  Yonder still spread the barren snow-choked fields ;
Over the cheerless lands white winter still
  His radiant sceptre wields.

But I dream strangely of some Orient calm
  Where this same sun drops west through stagnant
      heat,
While some swart Arab, near a drowsy palm,
  Lolls at his camel's feet.

III.

SHADOWS hung dense on the burnished lake
  Where our boat was languidly sliding ;
We heard in the forest the whip-poor-will wake,

And saw the red moon upgliding ;
And each told not, for the other's sake,
The sorrow that each was hiding.

We had wasted in passionate words and moods
The day that went down as our last ;
We had loitered in leafy solitudes
With the phantoms of our past !
Forgetting the grief in store for us
And the fate that followed fast,
Such radiant robe as it wore for us
From the present we had cast !
And now that the darkness fell again
Where our feet on the lit sward wandered,
We thought of the birds that sang in vain
And the sunbeams idly squandered !

Oh, better we did not speak—
That we looked at the shining shore,
At the clouded moon's far fiery streak,
At the dip of the glimmering oar !
Oh, better we did not seek
A voice for regret once more—
That we suffered, we silently bore !

I should not have pleaded one word
From your pale dear lips, or a sigh,
Had your soul gone then like a bird
From a rift in its prisoning bars !—
Ah, so thankfully watching you die,
Till your low voice was not heard
Nor your true heart longer stirred,
And the light of each fond eye
Had floated away to the stars !

IV.—ASTERS AND GOLDENRODS.

SUMMER, the dying queen, lay still,
And felt her weary heart grow chill
   With death's long lingering blight.
There, at brief distance from her gaze,
Two common weeds upreared their sprays
   In the sad sinking light.

Two wayside weeds that only knew
Those kind endearments that the dew
   The rain, the sunshine, make ;
.And though they looked of differing leaves,
Yet each was fraught with fragile sheaves
   Whose buds erelong would break.

Then the pale queen, in thankful pride,
Blessed these poor wildflowers ere she died,
   And said to them : " Behold,
Henceforth while here on earth ye live,
To one my purple robe I give,
   To one my crown of gold ! "

V.

ALL day the reapers on the hill
Have plied their task with sturdy will,
But now the field is void and still.

And wandering thither, I have found
The bearded spears in sheaves well-bound,
And stacked in many a golden mound.

And while cool evening suavely grows,
While o'er the sunset's dying rose
The first great white star throbs and glows,

While from the clear east, red of glare,
The ascendant harvest moon floats fair
Through dreamy deeps of purple air ;

While in among the slanted sheaves
A tender light its glamour weaves,
An elfish light that lures, deceives,

Then, swayed by fancy's dear command,
Amid the past I seem to stand,
In hallowed Bethlehem's harvest-land !

And through the vague field, dim-descried,
A homeward host of shadows glide,
And sickles gleam on every side.

Shadows of man and maid I trace,
With shapes of strength and shapes of grace,
Yet gaze but on a single face.

A candid brow, still smooth with youth ;
A smile of calm ; a mien of truth. . .
The patient star-eyed gleaner, Ruth !

VI.—TO A FRIEND WHO SLEPT ILL.

How hast thou angered into stern disdain
   That mild compassionate god round whose bowed
      head
The clustering poppies droop their drowsy red,
Somnus, that walks the world from twilight's wane
All the long night till day be born again, ·
   While after him, in shadowy legion, stream
   The pale diaphanous floating forms of dream ?

He kisses brows that ache from earthly care ;
   He soothes to peace the indignant souls of slaves ;
   O'er many an eye, grown tired with tears, he waves
Those rich-dyed languid flowers he loves to bear,
And yet for thee no tender spell doth spare,
   O friend that liest awake and hearest night
   Flow on past banks of time in stealthy might.

Ah, would that I, who am well-beloved of sleep,
   Might make fond intercession, friend, for thee,
   Each night when some shy Dream should visit me
Where the long labyrinths of slumber sweep !
Both the Dream's dim hands would I seize and keep,
   Praying of her to speed, with lulling charms,
   And wreathe about thy neck two rosy arms !

VII.

How long ere the blast that is nipping and bitter
  Shall blend with the bland air that tells winter's
    doom?
How long ere battalia of buttercups glitter?
  How long ere the tulip the terrace illume?
How long ere the young mating robin shall twitter,
  A gay-breasted flitter through vistas of bloom?

Come fleetlier, spring, for we languish to know thee
  Delaying no longer thy fairness afar!—
To see the sun burnish the smooth sward below thee,
  Or slant through the shower one long golden bar;
And watch the wild violets flocking to show thee
  What happy winds blow thee, in star after star.

VIII.—BABES IN THE WOOD.

SHE had two little babes, a boy and girl,
  Two little babes that are not with her now.
On one bright brow full golden fell the curl,
  The curl fell chestnut-brown on one bright brow.

She loves to dream of them that some soft day,
  While wandering far from home, their fitful feet
Went heedlessly along some woodland way
  Where shine and shade harmoniously meet;

And that they wandered deeper and more deep
  Into the forest's fragrant heart and fair,
Till just at evenfall they dropped asleep,
  And ever since they have been slumbering there.

After their wilful truantry, that day,
  Each is so tired it does not wake at all,
And over them the boughs that sigh and sway,
  Conspire to make perpetual evenfall.

And she, that must not join them, still is blest,
  However passionately her poor heart grieves;
For memories, like sweet birds at her behest,
  Have covered them with tender thoughts, like leaves!

IX.—AQUARELLE.

FAR away westward the cattle go,
  Dotting the land's dim edges;
Isled in the roseate afterglow,
  Darken the long cloud-ledges.   .

Burning each moment with warmer beams,
  Moon, by your sweet chaste power
Lull the world into lotus-dreams
  While you hang like a lotus-flower!

X.

How sad, in this wide airy glade,
  Where boughs with vocal tremor gleam,
Where great white clouds fling spots of shade
  And moons of timid daisies beam,
Near trilling bird and buoyant bee,
To find you thus, O gaunt dead tree!

Spectral you stand amid the glow
  And mirth in which you bear no part;
You hear the song, you feel the flow
  Of breezes fresh from summer's heart;
Yet still you know, with each glad breath,
The discongruity of death!

Oft through your dry stark frame will run
  Faint memories of fonder days;
Of fealty to the regnant sun
  And stately rapture in his rays;
Of how your live roots loved to coil
In mellow fathoms of cool soil.

Or yet about your sombre blight
  More tender dreams perchance may cling
Of how, with delicate delight,

Broke the first bud of your first spring,
And you in mute joy understood
Your own idyllic motherhood.

Or dearer still perchance you hold
    That hour when from your leafy breast
The first frail silver treble told
    Of downy young in your first nest,
And of its green protection proud,
Your vernal foliage laughed aloud.

Or you remember, it may be,
    In dumb and indeterminate way,
Some vine whose lithe fragility
    Clasped your strong bole and weakly lay
Fluttering against your vigor rude,
And charmed you with its gratitude.

But now no more you richly thrive;
    Alone yet not alone you reign,
As one alive yet not alive,
    A monument of patient pain;
While each new star the night makes clear
Moves you with separate souvenir.

Ah, best the sturdy woodman came
    And bore, ere winter gales could roam,

Your sapless wreck to cheer with flame
    The fireside of some peaceful home,
Till all your dumb regrets were lost
In sweet memorial holocaust !

XI.—CRADLE-SONG.

OH, slumber, my darling ; the white star is beaming
    From pale yellow dusk in the west.
Oh, slumber my darling ; with beautiful dreaming
    Its gleaming shall dower thy rest.

Oh, slumber, my darling ; the white star is glowing
    Leagues out on the shadowy sea,
And if the wild winds there be drearily blowing
    The knowing is not unto me.

Oh, slumber, my darling ; the white star in pillows
    Of purple-hued clouds sinks to sleep ;
This gale that is tossing the poor faded willows
    Wakes billows afar on the deep.

Oh, slumber, my darling ; the white star is dying,
    The gold autumn gloaming is dim ;
My thoughts to thy mariner father are flying,
    And sighing I fear me for him.

Oh, slumber, my darling ; the white star is beaming
   No longer, and low is the light.
Perchance where the grave of thy father is gleaming
   Are screaming the sea-gulls to-night !

XII.

THEY led the pale Christ through the mouthing
      throng,
   In Orient days far-fled ;
For then too often, as now, right cringed to wrong,
   And many had spoken and said :
      "Not this man, but Barabbas."

He was a thief, the pardoned one, 'tis writ :
   Did worse crime stain him red ?
Nay, thief or murderer—what mattered it ?
   For many had spoken and said :
      "Not this man, but Barabbas."

And so he walked unprisoned through the town ;
   And on the stern cross bled
The brow of Christ below the galling crown,
   For many had spoken and said :
      "Not this man, but Barabbas."

The world, forsooth, has learned its lesson well
  Since that dark hour and dread !
Full often accursed by the same bitter spell,
  Its lips have opened and said :
    "Not this man, but Barabbas."

XIII.

How marvellously all the deeps of night
  Make harmony with nature's many moods,
  Doming her oceans in their solitudes
With larger mystery and immenser might ;
Pouring pale glamours on the mountain's height ,
  Or quivering in the boughs of lonely woods ;
  Or where dead calm on some great desert broods,
With labyrinthine splendors throbbing white !

But oh, high stars what dissonance you bring
  When o'er the city, amid far narrower skies,
    You break like spectral flowers from magic seeds !
For then with sorrowing sovereignty you fling
  Your glory upon a million careless eyes
    Dragged earthward by innumerable greeds !

XIV.—To a Literary Fop.

You praise the poet of immortal name
  Now, when the world's best eulogies are willed him.
Living, he wanted bread far more than fame ;
  He was not "classic" till starvation killed him.

What if some Keats now felt the critic's brand ?
  Some Chatterton to-day cursed fortune's fetters ?
Dare you cheer either with benignant hand ?
  Not you !—sleek lacquey at the skirts of Letters !

XV.

Think not that you may calmly tread
  The loftier height that thousands miss,
Till you have measured all the dread
  And darkness of the abyss.

That foot which climbs where towers most high
  The peak of blended sun and snow,
Is always guarded by an eye
  That dares to look below !

XVI.

An old man mused, amid twilight's haze,
  While he watched a fading fire alone,
Which day of his long life's many days
  Could be named the fairest he had known.

Then out from his memory voices broke,
  And all were of days now past and dead ;
He smiled at forgotten dreams they woke
  In the low mellifluous words they said.

Of the grand Swiss mountains' power and peace,
  Of the Orient's lazy and splendid spell,
Of noons in Venice, of morns in Greece,
  Each day for its own sake pleaded well.

But when all the magic murmurs died
  Where his chamber drowsed in the spent logs'
    light,
" I was dim and cheerless," a new Day sighed,
  " I was chill with blast, I was bleak with blight,

" Yet I gave you that first warm poignant thrill
  When your first last love in your fond arms
    lay " . . .

"'Tis enough!" cried the old man. " Bleak and
    chill,
    You of all my days were the fairest day !"

XVII.

I saw in dreams a system of dead worlds,
Rolling, huge cinders, round a mightier sun,
Itself a cinder.   " Each world," said a voice,
" Was once, when millions of slow years had passed,
Glorious for beauty nature dowered it with,
But still more glorious for the habitants
That rose from ape to angel on its orb.
Then came, when millions of more years were spent,
Gradual extinction of the vast sun's fires   .   .
The system rolls to-day one mockery.   Look !"

Then in my dream I asked : " Will our sun fade
Like this, and all his courtier planets pale
Thus impotently ? "

                " Yes," the voice replied ;
" With worlds in space to evolve is to dissolve,
As even with us being born is but to die.
An individual immortality

Haunts with its hollow myth men's trusting hearts.
Forsake that shadow, and live thy human life
Nobly and adequately till the end."

"But if such end be nothingness?" I mourned.

"Then count thou on what flavorous opiates
This nothingness will brew thee.   Count thou, too,
On the soft unimaginable down
Its pillows hold for thee ; nor fail to think
How royaller than all earth's emperors
Man goes to his last rest who round himself
Doth wrap the draperies of eternity."

THE CARISFORT CURSE.

In the quiet Colonial years
Arthur Carisfort came overseas,
Here to build him a mansion that rose
From the heart of Virginia's wide woods.
Never statlier home had been seen,
Until now, below skies of our land ;
Never hallways and chambers more proud,
Never courtyard or terrace devised
With expansion more nobly diffuse.
From a hillside the lawns wavered green
Till they broke on a river's full flash,
And were merged, near its bank, in the peace
Of a village with gardens and streets
Almost calm as the greensward they met.
There alone through a decade of years,
Lingered Carisfort, wrapt, as it seemed,
In the charge of his one youthful child.

Many stories were told of the cause
Which had urged him from England, to dwell
So companionless but for the boy
Whom he treasured and guarded and taught.

Some avowed he was blighted in soul
By the blow of a widowing death ;
Others claimed that his life had been seared
By dishonor and anguish far worse ;
Others breathed of a treason acute
Which had made the King's axe graze his neck. . .
Still, the secret of why he had sought
Meditation and solitude, lay
Like a goblet or gem earth has hid
Under layers of oblivious dust.

Not a villager knew him for stern
When he passed with rare feet among men.
In his mien abode courtesy blent
With a sadness that lured while it chilled.
He was tall, yet of stature unbowed,
Though the hair to his temples clung white
As the locks of a brow twice his years.
Many deeds of sweet charity clad
With rich human aromas his name.
Only gossip's most poisonous mood
Found a sneer that could soil him, and this
Died in time of its own bitter sting.

Had they known him, these townsfolk, indeed,
How their hearts might with pity have pulsed !

Early wed to his cousin, who died
At the birth of the boy he so lŏved,
Fierce on Carisfort broke like a storm
Recognition of destiny's curse.
No recoiling ! the thing must be faced.
There he stood near the dead wife, his kin,
Whose last moments with madness were fraught.
Long ago in his youth, he had learned,
Vaguely heeding, of ancestors racked
By the same savage ill.   From his mind
Every vapor of doubt slowly crept.
Should he dwell here in England, or go
Where the sly push of sex in his blood
Might be smitten by loneliness dead ?
To his own heart he put question thus,
And the silence there thundered him " Go "   .
" Let me think not," heroic he mused,
" Of the grim fate that bans me and thralls.
Motes like mortals may rave at their dooms—
What avails it ?   Heredity's arm
Is a power that to thwart were to twist
The white bolt of the lightning in twain.
More than self, too, I shield this frail boy.   .   。
Whatsoe'er our progenitors did
In their dissolute bouts and amours,

They have left me my conscience at least,
And to make their dumb clay mine excuse
For desertion of duty, were shame
Such as cowards might clutch at, not I.
We, the last of the Carisforts, owe
Generations unborn holy debts.
They have called me an infidel here
In my brave Devon home, girt with ease ;
Let them learn not or learn, as fate wills,
How distrust of men's alterant creeds
May below it hide loyalty stanch
To the weal of a world packed with pains,—
Incorruptibly reaching toward right
As the pale wings of ships reach through dusk
Toward the patience of calm pilot stars."

So he mused, Arthur Carisfort ; so
He had made of his musings firm fact.
Year by year, from the funds of a brain
Long ere then stored with culture, he strove
To instruct and train Malcolm, his son.
And the boy, quick of wit, paid him well
For tuitions by love spurred and sped.
At eighteen, fair of face, large of limb,
Life for Malcolm was one giddy joy.

Through the mountains he rode hours alone,
Never dreaming of weariness. Weeks
Would elapse, yet he saw not a face
Save a few of his household. A heart
More replete with chaste innocence beat
Never yet in the breast of a boy.
All obedience, he sought not the town
Where it crouched at the stream's flashing curve.
"Go not there," said his father. The lad
Would have died ere he flouted such hest.

Peace abode at the great house, unstirred
By a faint wave of discord, straight on
Till befell Malcolm's twentieth year.
Then it chanced that one morning he met
Ruth Allaire, with the buttercup-gold
Of her curls, with the rose of her mouth,
As she strolled from the village to bear
Cheer and help for a woodlander's wife
Who lay dying. 'Twas June, and the leaves
Twinkled moist from the fresh roadside boughs.
Birds were warbling deliriums of song
To the sky's cloudless crystal, and airs
Full of odors and cadences roamed
Through the meadows and foliage as fond

As the hands of a bridegroom that steal
O'er the tresses and brows of his bride.

Just a gaze, and for Malcolm and Ruth
Speech was rosy necessity, love
Golden sequence, each quick in its course
As the glitters from dew struck by dawn.
Thus to meet was for warm youth like theirs
No less nature to meet yet again
Than if two stars from wide wastes of heaven,
Having once interblended stray beams,
Evermore should be brightly allied.

Now to Malcolm new life was alleged,
Half of happiness, half of remorse.
Many meetings with Ruth did he hold
In the dusk of dense oaks near the verge
Of the village, nor far from her home.
Like himself was the maiden sole child
Of a father as fond as his own.
Yet while one dwelt austerely aloof,
One was loved for his wealth of kind works,
Eager sympathies, taintless ideals,—
A Virginian of that nobler mould
War and time have annulled, living now
But in chronicle's dim-pictured page.

Then at last, with the truth on his lips,
With a heart throbbing guiltily quick,
To his father went Malcolm, one eve,
In the dark-panelled room where he sat
Near a lamp shining clear on his book.
" I would speak with you," murmured the youth ;
" I would tell of unduteous deceits."   ·

Round his neck in an instant he felt
The embrace of his father.   " My boy,
Do not hesitate ; leave nothing hid.
It was better—far wiser—to seek
Full confession, as thus.   Tell me all."

So enjoined, with glad candor that leapt
From that soilless young spirit enshrined
In the grace, height and health of his frame,
Unreluctant of detail, right on,
Full of penitence yet well devoid
Of humility suppliant or veiled,
In his rich eager voice Malcolm spoke.

Not a syllable Carisfort missed ;
Not a meaning, or shade of one, slipped
From his calm but intense mood of heed.

Then at last, when the tale had been told,
White and silent he stared at his son.

"Oh, my father," cried Malcolm, aghast
At the change his avowals had wrought,
" Pray you, speak! Have I angered you ?"

"No!"

As he heard, Malcolm shuddered, so bleak
Did the dominant utterance float
On the absolute stillness.   .   .

Erelong,
With his look unfamiliar and wild,
Flashed the next words from Carisfort, full
Of the fierce love brutes keep for their kind.

" Not in anger! Nay, boy, light of life,
Star of cheer, bloom of hope, son more sweet
To my bosom than rain to sere grass,
Not in anger! Yet heavenly as love
Such as mine, it ordains, it commands
With a voice that is worldlier than sin !
All the fault is not yours ; I have erred
In my custody, fond though its aims !"

Then he told of the curse that for years
Had o'ershadowed the Carisfort name.
Not a detail he spared ; his discourse,
Like the glass of a wizard, lured out
From remoteness of ancestry shapes
Diabolic or piteous or gross.
To the whitening cheek of his son
Came the witness of pain and dismay.
Yet he crushed all compassion ; the truth
Now too tardily spoke, must be bared,
Though its nudity, hideous as hate,
Were a torture to him that beheld.

So at length, having swept through the dark
Of disconsolate annals like these,
To the pale boy said Carisfort " Choose
If the viperous evils I name
Shall be fed with new life from your blood !
Here is peace, in the home I have built
For your pleasure through years yet to be.
What is love but a madness, at most ?
All of life that is choicest lies hid
In the leaves yonder bookshelves enshrine.
But the glorious and mutable hills,
With a steed that shall rival the wind,

These are yours, O my Malcolm, as well !   .   .
What is love but a madness, at most ?"

Then the boy answered, " Father, no, no !
Were the house you have built here a hall
Full of grandeur kings covet, my heart
Could but hate it if shared not with *her !*
Surely never till now have I known
Half the meaning of solitude.   Now
Neither meadow nor mountain may lend ˙
Sweet companionship just as of old,
But in every fair phase of each one
I discern a mysterious defect,—
Shy, elusive, at first, yet when found.
Speaking only her absence !   How, then,
Could I pass years that reft me of Ruth ?
Better death, were it coiled in the balm
Of her kiss, like a worm in ripe fruit !"

"Worse than death," said his father, " were life
Such as this you demand.   Ah, my lad,
In her kiss lurks a woe that may waste
With its ravage your children and hers !
Have I taught you so latally ill
That you dare turn from duty's deep eyes
When they front you so steadfast as now ?

See—your own yea or nay shall resolve
If through long lines of beings unborn
You perpetuate sorrow like pest,
Or destroy it through stanch rule of self."

Into Malcolm's clear look stole the light
Of rebellion, its breath curled his lip.

" No, my father.   Since nature decrees
I should cloister not spirit and sense
Amid abstinence, penance, retreat,
Far the wiser, I judge it, to bow
Mine obeisance, nor thwart nature's will."

" You defy me, then, Malcolm ? "

                              " Not so.
I revere you as always, but feel
That a power I may name not compels
From your counsels my purpose,— though firm
In its dear filial troth stays my love ! "

" As you please," rang from Carisfort.   " Go !
Nay, no hand-clasp nor kiss for good-night !
On the morrow, sir—— Oh, my poor boy !
Since you seek it, here—here, as of yore,

To this breast that your young gold of hair
Hath been pillowed so oft by ! "

                    His voice,
Full of obdurate rigors at first,
Soon had melted with fatherhood.   Close
Once again, for a brief while, he clasped
In his arms the astonished boy ; then,
With release and a hand-wave that meant
" Pray you, leave me," he sought his desk, there
Low to bend o'er its big lamplit book.

But when Malcolm had passed from the room
He arose, and with gesture abrupt,
From a casement swept back the still folds
Of its tapestries, baring to view
An immense bulk of mountain that seemed
Like a vast ocean-billow some spell
Hath made immobile ; darkly it curved
In its majesty, mystery and grace,
Below beams of the large vernal moon.

" O inscrutable night," mused this man,
" How you look your indifference divine
On mortality's pathos of pain !
Many millions ere I have gazed forth

At your infinite beauty, to find
Uncompassionate absence of help.
We that toil with the tangle of life
May but seek its unravelment here
In the silence our human souls hoard.
And while seeking it thus, how we fail !
Yet there comes to us all, if we cast
Underfoot every impulse of self,
Some response we may cling to and trust,
Though its tidings be torture !   I gain
From the oracle fearful command.
Shall I heed it ?   Why not ?   To recoil
In disdain of it only may mean
The continuance, age after age,
Of a race racked with malady dire.
Shall I dare let this wrong fester on ?
What's morality ?   Service to men
By each leal individual man.
Metaphysics may mould from its fogs
This or that fair fantastical shape
Transcendental believers adore.
My philosophy pauses devout
At the lintels of reason ; my love
Kneels at altars philanthropy builds.
When the ravening cancer frets flesh

'Tis the cold knife of science that cures,
Not the herb superstition hath culled.
Science reigns. . .   'Twas astrology, once,
Haughty stars, icy moon, that ye faced.
'Tis astronomy now—weak, I own,
To decipher your whither and whence,
Yet a millionfold mightier, truth knows!
Good from evil?   Religion's glib lie!
Good and evil are foes hot with hate.
Who engendered them?   God?   Wherefore, then?
Did he make them to mar with their feuds
This humanity needless to make
Save as angels, his glorious caprice
And the replica grand of himself?
Nay, my god is mankind; *he* will delve
Through creations dark fundaments; he
Will twist fingers round obstinate roots,
Disentangle mysterious coils,
In the black reek of poison plant balm,
Tear diseases like weeds from the blood,
Knead to harmony civic disputes,
Turn the planet millennial—when all
That now breathe on it long have lain dust.
Yet this dazzling accomplishment lags
Through indefinite centuries; we,

Born so soon on a mere infant world,
Can but serve as purblind pioneers
For its future magnificence.   Most
That we do is frail, tentative, yet
By some poor pulse of effort we still
May allege ourselves duteous and fine—
Not the sluggards who take life as brutes
Take a bone betwixt gluttonous teeth.
I'll do *my* share, at least.   .   .   Ah, they knew,
Those old Romans,—Virginius that smote
The white paps of his desecrate girl,
And rough Brutus, who flared on the mob
Slain Lucretia   .   .   *they* died for ideas !
Let me die so—and he, my sweet boy ! "

O'er the casement flung Carisfort, now,
Its voluminous curtain.   The room
For a moment seemed absolute dark,
Till aloof, burning tranquil, he saw
From his desk the familiar lamp shine
Which had glimmered so many a night
On the pages he read in old tomes
Rich with musings of seers long entombed.

In a brief while his visage had grown
Drawn, cadaverous.   .   .   Moving as one

Half unconscious, he trod hall or stair,
And at last by the bed of his boy,
White and stirless he waited.   No sign
Save of slumber's benignant control.
From a window unshaded, the moon
Smote with delicate splendor the brow,
Throat and lips of the sleeper.   He smiled,
And the smile seemed a silvery ghost
Of some flower that in gardens of dream
Hath unfolded its petals for Love
While it walks there to pause and behold,
With its arm round the warm neck of Youth.

"Let him die so.   .   .   I envy his death."

This from Carisfort, hardly more said
Than 'twas thought.   On a knife that he drew,
Flashed the moonlight.   .   .   No cry left the boy ;
All too merciful shot the sure blow.

   * * * * * *

At the village, that night, cries arose
When a mist hued like blood scaled the heaven.
What was this leapt so fearful afar ?
Was the Carisfort homestead ablaze ?
In a tumult they rushed, boys and men—
Women, too, though past midnight the hour.

When the first hardy runner attained
The great structure, its doom had been sealed.
Well had Carisfort planned his wild scheme .   .
For from basements and attics alike
Did profuse jets of scarlet outpour,
And a gaunt lurid column of smoke
From the main roof was towering august.

To an awestricken mob soon had swelled
They that stared on the hungry turmoil.
Like a shadowy accomplice, the wind
Sped with fleet volatility here,
There and everywhere, kindling the greed
Of combustion, as hate kindles crime.

" Look—the North wing ! " a shout rang from some,
And in hurrying wonder all sped
Where the North wing stood shrouded with fire.
At a casement—one moment, no more—
Like a phantom gleamed Carisfort.   Close
To his breast he had gathered a form
That was limp as if lifeless. .   .   He stooped,
And with eager lips pressed the slant cheek.   .   .
Then a scorpion of flame writhed its way
To the casement, and watchers beheld
In its place one red frenzy of glare.

When the dawn with reluctant pearl pushed
From horizon to zenith, it showed
In the mansion's proud place fuming bulks
Of charred rafter and dislocate stone.

But the Carisfort curse was annulled.
Nevermore by this race would be reaped
That implacable harvest of pain
Which "the sins of the parents" had sown.

AGNOSTIC AND CHRISTIAN.

CHRISTIAN.

No bigot heart is in my breast ;
   Though creeds may clash, I do not care ;
The certitude that brings me rest
   Is rosier than auroral air.
I know that gain will follow loss,
   That after suffering peace will come ;
I know Christ hung upon his cross
   For me, in matchless martyrdom.

AGNOSTIC.

These things you know ?   Yet knowledge owns
   True birth from hardier force than faith ;
In hills and meadows, brooks and stones,
   Dwells flimsy fancy's hovering wraith.
What sways your soul with easy breath
   Makes impious adamant of mine.
No Lazarus ever rose from death ;
   No water changed itself to wine !

CHRISTIAN.

The Almighty, whose least edict awes,
   May work such mandate as he wills ;

From him the effect, from him the cause,
  The storms and calms, the goods and ills.
We are born, live, die, at his command;
  He reigns eternally sublime;
In the vast hollow of his hand
  He holds us till the end of time.

AGNOSTIC.

Mark well the world wherein we bide,
  Its pangs of misery, want, disease.
Is this Lord thou hast glorified
  The untrammeled arbiter of these?
Do hospitals that moan with pain,
  Do haunts where madness yells and leers,
Attest the triumph of his reign
  In liturgies of pangs and tears?

CHRISTIAN.

He brings the blight, the curse, the ban;
  He brings the blessing, joy or hope.
With his incomparable plan
  Our mortal ken would vainly cope.
He asks us but to kneel devout
  Before the wisdom of his ways,—
To drown the assailant sins of doubt
  In lowly plenitudes of praise.

AGNOSTIC.

How stern the tyrannies you paint !
  His curling lash may deal us woes,
Yet we, who are smitten till we faint,
  Must bow unmurmuring to its blows.
And praise ?   What need of praise or blame
  Hath he from our brief human term ?
Though you might crush it dead, you claim
  No hallalujahs from the worm.

CHRISTIAN.

We cannot meet on common ground ;
  For me mankind with wonder shook
When first it learned that love profound
  Which fills one mighty and sacred Book.
To those pure pages, young yet old,
  All promise, grace or pardon clings ;
I turn them, and I hear unfold
  The pale plumes of celestial wings.

AGNOSTIC.

A book by random piecemeal wrought
  From wandering fables dimly spelt,
Ere yet even mediæval thought
  Had made its timorous twilights felt.

A book whose choicer texts are big
  With rhapsodies of mystic phrase,
By sage, grammarian, gownsman, prig
  Interpreted in myriad ways. .

Or yet a book where battle and gore
  Flare crude as lessons charged with cheer—
Where some red coarse Jehovah's roar
  Tears reverence from the cringe of fear ;
Where slavery is to honor wed,
  Polygamy rank baseness feeds ;
Where vengeance counts its bloody dead,
  And mercy is throttled while it pleads !

A book that such raw wrath delights,
  That such hot outrages o'erflow,
As Moses wrought the Midianites,
  As Joshua poured on Jericho.
A book whose God oped nostrils wide
  For fumes of burning ox and sheep,
His paltry power being pacified
  When Pharaoh slaughtered babes in sleep !

CHRISTIAN.

Sneer, if you wish, at tales like those,
  Where dream with history may have blent,

Yet spare the immortal word that grows
   From Apostolic Testament ;
It stays a joy no jar may shock,
   A surety of holy rest, release,
A dovecote round whose doorways flock
   Flute-throated doves with eyes of peace.

He came, He wrought, He bled, He died,
   For you, for me, for all men born,
Till gloriously beatified
   He rose on resurrection-morn.
And ah, since then his memory glows
   Like lamps of help through storm's dark stress,
Or fire of that red blood which flows
   Hot from the heart of righteousness.

Above the ironic scoff, above
   The lustiest hate cold logic gives,
For nigh two thousand years of love
   His testimony untarnished lives.
Though soft they rang, those words He spake
   Were leashed with echoes loud and free,
Still buoyed on all the winds that wake,
   Still regnant in the unrestful sea !

Why did not Christ, if God indeed,
   Behold the future clear-unfurled,
With feuds that in his name would breed
   Their wild disasters on the world?
Why saw he not how wrangling sects
   Would soon his meek ideals beslime,—
How dogmatism would turn his texts
   To bannered shibboleths of crime?

Below cathedrals towering strong,
   That hailed him with aerial spires,
He must have heard what shrieks erelong
   Would peal from faction's greedy pyres.
All persecution's direst pains
   Omniscience like his own foreknew—
Fierce Torquemada's racks and chains,
   Or frenzy of St. Bartholomew.

To-day, when reason's poignant flame
   Has lit the paths where blindness trod,
It should be intellectual shame
   To grant that Christ was one with God.
Howe'er tradition's tongue may prate,
   Belief its faded embers fan,

That man hath less of manlier weight
   Who holds that Christ was more than man !

CHRISTIAN.

Allow no grim calumnious trace
   Be found your bitter speech to stain,
What wretched gloom would wrap the race
   Were trust in sweet redemption slain !
Oh, call the dawn the day's dull close,
   The lily a harlot, if you will,
But leave to prayer that rich repose
   Its Heavenward incense can distil !

How should we dare through life to go,
   If last and first it should express
The unmeaning prelude played to show
   A drama of dreary nothingness ?
How should we dare, like aimless fools,
   Build purposes of moral might,
Were these but splendid vestibules
   To chaos and eternal night ?

Off sovereign faith once rudely tear
   The purple and sceptre it has known,
And pagan sensualism will glare
   Like a new Nero's from its throne !

Ah, once let mortal minds hold vain
   What shelter of pardon they could win,
And blasphemy strikes up the strain
   Despair goes dancing to with sin !

AGNOSTIC.

That loftier fortitude I bless
   Which rates all creeds as empty strife,
Yet dares be duteous, none the less,
   To every large demand of life.
I envy not the ethic range
   Of him whose virtues would require
That wrong and right should interchange
   For so much Heaven like so much hire.

Look firm on death, our common lot ;
   Fare near it with unfaltering gait ;
Die like the patriot soldier, not
   The dullard mercenary of fate.
Nor deem philanthropy hath laws
   To dole thee pay like sordid pelf ;
Love thou thy fellow-man because
   To hate him were to soil thyself !

Raze church and temple ; worship kill ;
   Strike all religions till they reel ;

Humanity is an altar, still,
   Where man may reverently kneel.
In acts of high unsullied worth
   Lives all of Heaven our souls may guess ;
The only atheist here on earth
   Is he that scorns their godliness !

KATE ROMNEY.

(Coast of New England.)

THE white waves broke on the dusky rocks as the tide
    swept up from the harbor-bar,
And journeying gulls went by in flocks, with a scream
    to the vesper star.

Across the meadows Kate Romney came, and saw
    while the air turned chill and gray,
The lights in her mother's cottage flame, far off by the
    windy bay.

The dreary tones of the tide had borne a meaning
    sweet to her maiden ear.
" You shall wed," they sang, " by to-morrow morn with
    the lover you hold so dear ! "

On a sudden, then, as she glided past, a hand in the
    dimness caught her own.
Like an iron gyve it held her fast, by the breaker's
    deepening moan.

" Is it you, Mark—you ? " faint-voiced she said, cowed
    low at the pitiless look he wore.
" Does the sea in truth give up her dead ? Do their
    wan ghosts haunt its shore ?

Are you ghost or man ? . . . For he did not speak,
    while the tides crawled near, to gird them round.
As pale as the pale waves grew her cheek, but the
    strong hand firmly bound.

She read her doom in his stubborn eye ; she thought
    of lover, of kin, of home . .
They stood in the loudening surge breast-high, encom-
    passed with ghostly foam.

"O pity the fault of a broken vow ! Your ship came
    not, and I thought you dead !" . .
Then he spoke, and the noisy waters, now, reached up
    for the words he said.

"At last I have come, and all is well ! They shall
    part us no more, these winds and waves,
Till God has sounded His judgment-knell, and the
    great sea bares her graves !"

INCONGRUITIES.

I.

I LOOKED within the colorless face, last night,
  Of one for whom life promised, when he went,
  The alluring fruit of rich accomplishment—
One dowered to find rare favor in the sight
Of all who set their spirits toward the light;
  One molded to be nobly eminent.
    Yet ah! that in this great sweet heart should
      glide
    The subtle and fatal curse, too late espied! . .
    He pressed the pistol to his brow, and died!

I meet amid my walk, from day to day,
  A little faded man, low-bowed with years.
  From him time's tyrannies, that disdain men's tears,
Health, kindred, wealth and friends have stolen away.
And yet to its hopeless aching crumbling clay
  His tired-out soul with stubborn clutch adheres.   .
    O human life! thou sphinx, whose haughty will
    Forever through the ages gives us still
    These baffling riddles that we solve so ill! .

II.

THERE were two men, each greatly loathing each,
  Because of battling interests and the greed

For goals of rule that either strained to reach,
  And rivalry of differing aim and deed.
And both won much, though either failed to fall,
  And still each loathed his fellow till the last;
Nor did their great hates pass away at all
  Till either's power to loathe or love was past.

And after? . . Why, their tombs' old sculptured
    pride
Rise in the regal abbey, side by side,
Where friends devoutly laid them when they died.

There was a man that loved a woman well,
  Even loved with so all-dominant a fire
That only thus could he make language tell
  The depth and breadth and height of his desire :
" When we are dead, pray Heaven that either lies
  In graves whose mantling grasses intertwine !
For were we laid apart, my dust would rise
  And die again that it might rest by thine!"

And after? . . Why, the woman sleeps to-day,
Dreamless and easeful, under graveyard clay.
Where sleeps her love ? The immense sea does not
    say !

THE MILKY WAY.

ABOVE me, in solemn skies that clouds have left
  A dreamy infinitude of throbbing light,
Faint as diaphanous vapor, it has cleft
  With shadowy causeway the blue voids of night.

I lift my gaze, by silent reverie won,
  And nothing then the aerial fancy mars
That spirits in silver wizardry have spun
  Some pale miraculous cobweb through the stars !

But science, on dauntless wings that never close,
  The stately mystery like a veil has torn,
And shown us, quivering with deep natal throes,
  A terrible embryo of worlds unborn.

Here chaos lurks, in many a wild vague ring,
  And laboring spheres rebel from its embrace,
Age after age victoriously to swing
  Out through the opaque enormities of space.

Ah! where sublime these nebulous wreaths hang
    curled,
  May one star wake to being, if one alone,
Fit grandly to be named a perfect world,
  Freed from the sin, the agony of our own !

HISTORY.

He that the record of mankind would trace,
  With all its virtues, faults, hopes, passions, fears,
  In hardier scripture than a few fleet years
To dull oblivion may at last efface,
  Must plunge his look far deeper than of old
  Among time's ruinous heaps of dross and gold.

For every potentate, whate'er his pride,
  Bows to still mightier forces, dim, remote ;
  His very tyrannies, like his mercies, float
As wandering foam on the vast human tide
  That sleeps or swings in that mysterious flood
  Wrought red and bounteous from a nation's blood.

Ye, therefore, whom profounder truth contents
  Than babble of light court-lady, prince or page,
  Tell how through altering peoples, age by age,
Great causes fructified in great events,
  Nor heed mere kings, with splendors frail and
    brief,—
  Frederick the Greedy, Bonaparte the Thief !

ENNUI.

Amid luxurious ease and splendid state
She languished, bitterly disconsolate;
  She felt the massive grandeur of the crown
  Weigh all her tired young spirit sternly down
Beneath its ponderous and enfeebling weight.

She loathed her pageantries in hall or street;
Her vassal throngs; her coach's gilded seat;
  Her statesmen and proud warriors when they came,
  Allegiantly forgetful of their fame.
Kneeling in duteous fealty at her feet.

The wandering story-tellers, they that had
So subtle a skill to make despondence glad;
  The grave court-leeches that with looks of gloom
  Held converse in her silent ante-room;
The tinkling hunchback jester, gaudy-clad;

Her woods, in whose green wilds the boar was chased;
Her porphyry fountains, with rare sculptures graced;
  Her palace towers that nobly dared the day,
  With dizzy crests where broidered flags hung gay;
Her lofty terraces where the peacocks paced;

Or yet through shadowy grove and ferny glade,
With lords and ladies in rich pomp arrayed,

With tasselled steeds and falcons fluttering white,
Banners and plumes and poursuivants in sight,
The passing of her radiant cavalcade !

She loathed them all with strength she could not speak,
And in her carven chair, week after week,
Low she would bow her head and dumbly brood,
While from the prisoning velvet of her snood
The long blond braid fell out on her pale cheek.

And once, 'tis said, a minstrel, known for art
To appease with song the melancholy heart,
Craved gracious audience of this drooping queen.
'Twas given ; but when he came with humble mien,
Moved by strange whim, she bade her dames depart.

And now the minstrel swept his harp to sing
Melodious eulogy, so mild of ring
It wavered heavenward in the same sweet wise
As those gray odorous vapors when they rise
From silvery censers that the priesthood swing.

But here his listener cries, with brows that lower :
" Tell me no more of my own worth and power !
I weary to the bone of flattery's lies !
Speak out some rank truth,. naked of disguise !
Mock me—insult me !—or you die this hour ! "

ILLEGITIMACY.

(Spoken in a Prison-Cell.)

I ROBBED you amid the crowd
    While the play sent forth its throng.
Let the wrong be all avowed,
    If it was indeed a wrong.
You came when you read my message? Well,
You are welcome here, in this dull cell.

With want (and with envy, too)
    I was sick to the very bone ;
And yet when I stole from you
    'Twas because of yourself alone,
As you passed me in the crowds thick press.
With your handsome superciliousness !

I had known you for years by sight. . .
    Let the bitter truth be told. . .
My poor dead mother, one night,
    First pointed you out of old.
Your lighted windows looked on the street
Where we two watched amid whistling sleet.

The lacqueys, by some mischance,
    Had left the curtains undrawn ;
You romped in a wild glad dance,

Like a lovely and restless fawn.
You were six years old, all mirth and grace,
With no pride yet in your rosy face.

Rich carpets and mirrors clear
    Gleamed round you in lavish pomp;
Your stately father stood near
    And smiled as he saw you romp,
And spoke now and then with loving air
To the wife at ease in her tufted chair.

My mother grew deathly white
    While she watched the glowing room.
I can see her, on that drear night,
    Through the sleety and windy gloom
Stretching out her wasted fingers, red
From toil with the needle, as she said:

" One reared amid splendors there;
    One having not even a name!
One tended with dainty care;
    One cursed with hunger and shame!"
What strange hard words for a child were those!
Yet I've understood them since, God knows!

THE ICICLE.

DON LORENZO.
DOÑA AMALIA.
ANITA, *a duenna.*

(*Seville : an open room, with veranda at back, and the
Guadalquiver seen dimly.* DOÑA AMALIA *at
embroidery frame.* DON LORENZO *on a couch,
with head and one limb in bandages.*)

AMALIA.

O TIRESOME roses, how your patterns linger
Before my craft can shape them as I will !
Poor gentleman, he sleeps ?   (I've pricked my finger !)
Poor gentleman, he sleeps inertly still !

(*She sees a slight movement in* DON LORENZO, *and droops head.*)

LORENZO.

Cold girl, that all the gossips here in Seville
Have called " the icicle," as well they might,
How quickly you would send me to the devil
If conscious of my true deceitful plight !

AMALIA (*with finger on lip*).

How strange!   He spoke!   I'd swear to it—or nearly
   Ah, he's but talking in his sleep, of course.
Unhappy gentleman, you've paid severely
   For riding an unmanageable horse!

(ANITA *enters, with sherbet.*)

Less noise, Anita!   What a step you tread with!

ANITA.

He sleeps?

AMALIA.

            Well, not so soundly as I thought.   .
But you've a footfall one could wake the dead with!

(*Tastes sherbet.*)

   Ah, what a poor weak sherbet you have brought

ANITA.

Nay, señorita, I was never skillful
   At tasks like these; their art I ne'er could learn.
Go thou, dear child, and brew a better gill-ful;
   I'll watch the gentleman till thou return.

AMALIA.

So be it, Anita.   Are you quite decided
   He needs no doctor?

ANITA.

Doctors all be . . blest
He'll soon get well and strong enough, provided
His bruises may secure sufficient rest.

AMALIA.

Well, well, I leave him in your charge, Anita ;
Do gently whatsoever he may bid. . .

ANITA.

You speak so of *a man !*—you, *favorita !*

AMALIA.

He's not a real man ; he's an . . invalid !
(*Exit* AMALIA.)

LORENZO (*springing up from couch*).

Never till now, in sooth, did Spanish gentle
Light on duenna that was half so good !
Ah, your benevolence is monumental ;
I'd canonize you if I only could !

ANITA.

May the Saints pardon thy blaspheming twitter !
I've been most rashly wicked !

LORENZO.

Nay, you've not !

ANITA.

Oh, yes !   Her eyes have such a truthful glitter ;
  They pierce me with repentance.

LORENZO.

                              And for what ?
Is it because this venturing spirit chooses
  To seek thus boldly my affianced wife ?

ANITA.

Affianced, if you will ; but she refuses
  All other future save a loveless life !

LORENZO.

Bah, dame !   A stale fig for her freaks of fancy
  I come from Cordova to claim my bride !

ANITA.

Then you must win her by a necromancy
  Whose magic shall work marvels with her pride.

LORENZO.

Fear not ; I'll do it, nurse !

ANITA.

                              Poor orphan, truly
  Her fate is hard, with both dear parents dead !

LORENZO

My fate is harder, that I've this unruly
Andalusian maid to woo and wed.

ANITA.

Thou followest thine own reckless choice!

LORENZO.

How? Grumbling?
Good nurse, your mood has turned most wry indeed!

ANITA.

Nor strange!—with thine imaginary tumbling
To earth from that imaginary steed!

LORENZO.

Deception villanous—I grant it!

ANITA.

Waiting
In ambush, I must aid thy sorry guile!—
Assist thee past our threshold, hotly hating
Such fraudulent behavior all the while!

LORENZO (*drooping head*).

True—true!

ANITA.

And when my lady at length had seen us,
I with untold hypocrisy must say,
"Ah, señorita, shall we seek, between us,
    This gentleman's discomforts to allay?"

LORENZO.

And she!   How beautiful was her compassion!
    Shams though my bruises were, they ached, I'll
        swear!

ANITA.

You merit aching in a different fashion!

LORENZO.

Come, now, your spleen and not your heart spoke
    there!

(*Takes out purse.*)

Good nurse, that struggling son in Salamanca—
    The barber with eight children . . .

ANITA (*refusing purse*).

                    Say no more!

LORENZO.

That daughter, then—the sailor's wife, Bianca,
    Dwelling in Barcelona. . .

ANITA.

Nay, señor!

LORENZO.

So of my proffered gold hast thou proved wary
  Since first to win my way with thee I tried!
Who dares to call duennas mercenary?
  Lope de Vega—Calderon—you have lied!

ANITA.

Your thoughts of me are sure one precious tangle,
  Thus low my loyal services to rate!
I'm not the sort of fish, howe'er you angle,
  That cares to nibble at a golden bait.
I want the lady I love to marry wisely
  A nobleman of breeding, heart and head!

LORENZO.

Your sentiments consort with mine precisely;
  I, too, in just that way would have her wed!

ANITA.

Here's impudence, forsooth!

LORENZO.

But you condone it!

ANITA.

All the world loves a lover, as they say. . .

LORENZO.

I'm hers !—in rapt allegiance, nurse, I own it,
   And pant to have her name our nuptial day !

ANITA.

Then rashly has thine adoration reckoned ! . .
   Still does her beauty feed its amorous glow ?

LORENZO

Saint Simon Stylites, if she beckoned,
   Would leave his pillar and play Romeo !

ANITA.

More blasphemy !

LORENZO

       On *Las Delicias* walking,
I first idealized her—*ay de mí !*
   But now !—her lips would set a dumb man talking !
Her eyes have beams to make a blind man see !

ANITA.

Nay, but her proud young bosom cannot shelter
   One gleam of answering passion, warm or chill !
She's a real icicle !

LORENZO.

       But I can melt her !

ANITA.

Alas ! impossible !

LORENZO.

I can—and will !

ANITA.

No, I defy thee !

LORENZO.

When I'm once defeated,
Sound forth at pleasure your victorious drums !

ANITA.

Pray heaven by false impressions I've been cheated !

LORENZO.

Amen, nurse !

ANITA.

Quick—be ill again ! .   .   She comes !

(Doña Amalia *re-enters with sherbet.* Don Lorenzo
has resumed his place on couch, closing his eyes.)

AMALIA.

Does he still sleep ?

ANITA.

I think he does, *carina.* . .

AMALIA.

Let us not wake him, then, whate'er we do !

(*Puts sherbet on table beside couch.*)

It seems to me, nurse, I have seldom seen a
   More healthful-looking sick man. . . Pray, have
      you ?

ANITA.

Indeed, he *hath* more color, now I scan him,
   Than most sick gentlemen I've seen before.
But then the accident that did unman him
   Occurred so suddenly. . .

(DON LORENZO *snores.*)

AMALIA.

What's that ?

ANITA.

A snore.

AMALIA.

'Twas most unmusical !   Ah, saints preserve us !
   It may perchance have been a groan of pain !

LORENZO (*feigning sleep*).

Oh, beautiful Amalia !

ANITA.

Don't be nervous.

AMALIA.

He's talking in his sleep?

ANITA.

'Tis more than plain.

AMALIA.

He called me beautiful!

ANITA.

Well, there's no fiction.

AMALIA.

Still, the impertinence acutely stings!

ANITA.

Child, when we sleep we pay no care to diction;
We naturally say all sorts of things.

AMALIA.

Oh, you believe he meant it not? Still, clearly
His words were spoke. They did not seem obscure.

LORENZO.

If she's an icicle, it must be merely
That while she's radiant she is also pure!

AMALIA.

He calls me "icicle." He must have known me
Ere now,—perchance even weeks, or months, or
more!

LORENZO.

Would that unamiable brute had thrown me
A little nearer to my loved one's door !

AMALIA.

His loved one's door !

ANITA.

Quite strange !

AMALIA.

It makes me shiver !
I'll wake him, nurse ; I ——

ANITA.

Oh, tut, tut !   For shame !

LORENZO.

How sweet to think the same sweet Guadalquivir
By Cordova and Seville winds the same !

AMALIA.

Just hear !

LORENZO.

Now mine has been the boundless pleasure
To feel such beauty and grace my spirit stir,
That silvery stream henceforward I shall treasure
All the more fondly since it flows near her !

AMALIA.

Wake him, nurse, wake him !

ANITA.

Wake him thou, if willing

LORENZO.

The right was mine to pass below her roof,
Yet, fearful that she would prove proudly chilling,
I, Count of Alvaredo, stood aloof.

AMALIA.

Lorenzo, Count of Alvaredo !

ANITA (*picking up a handkerchief*).

Look you . . .

This kerchief bears the Alvaredo crest !

AMALIA (*recoiling*).

That man of all men !

(*Rushes impetuously toward couch.*)

ANITA.

Have your wits forsook you ?

The shock might kill him !

AMALIA (*calmer*).

Leave us, then ; 'tis best.

I, when he wakes, have something, nurse, to utter
That fitlier would be told were we alone.
Go, therefore.

ANITA.

You appear in curious flutter ;
The voice you speak with has an alien tone.

AMALIA.

No matter ; go !

ANITA (*aside*).

Her eyes like fireflies glisten !
Pray heaven I shall not rue this day with tears !
I'm tempted at the keyhole now to listen ;
But ah, time stuffs with cotton these old ears !

(*Exit* ANITA).

AMALIA.

How strange !   The Count of Alvaredo lying
Hurt in *my* house, dependent on *my* aid,
And while he sleeps, preposterously sighing
Nonsense too silly for a masquerade !

LORENZO (*feigning to awake*).

I trust I've talked not in my sleep ?

AMALIA.

Well .   .   slightly.

LORENZO.

Then pray have I said aught to hurt or vex ?

AMALIA.

Naught of least moment, if I heard you rightly .   .
Only the usual babble of your sex.

LORENZO.

Ah, lady, and so you like not men ?

AMALIA.

I deem you
A race of monarchs,—in your own conceit !
Gracious to women—who as gods esteem you !
  Courteous to women—who will kiss your feet !
We are prized and petted—while our beauty lingers,
  Respected, reverenced—while we chance to please,
Then tossed away, as with contemptuous fingers
  You toss your cigarillos to the breeze !

LORENZO.

Pray what stern cynic taught you that our dealings
  With woman were thus flagrant past excuse ?

AMALIA.

Flagrant ?   Oh, I've no words to phrase my feelings !

LORENZO.

No words ?   I thought them notably profuse.

AMALIA.

So, you're satirical !

LORENZO.

Nay, simply truthful.

AMALIA (*with scorn*).

You'd like more flippancy?   I seem too grave?

LORENZO.

No, you're as picturesque as you are youthful;
Rave on; it so becomes you when you rave.

AMALIA.

Señor, I did not seek your admiration;
Detest me, if you wish, with eager zest.

LORENZO.

There's no use asking for my detestation;
You're far too entertaining to detest.

AMALIA.

I beg you, Don Lorenzo, not to squander
Flatteries on *me* !

LORENZO.

You've learned the name I bear.

AMALIA (*confused*).

My old duenna found your kerchief yonder,
And knew the crest of Alvaredo there.

LORENZO.

Alas, you are right! How vain the proud regalia
  Of all my rank and caste!

AMALIA.

Why call it vain?

LORENZO.

Know you a lady of Seville named Amalia
  Del Castro?—of the bluest blood in Spain?

AMALIA (*greatly embarrassed*).

Yes . . I have seen the lady. . . At least I
    think so. . .
  One knows a bevy of people here—by sight.

LORENZO.

I love her madly—intensely! . . Wherefore shrink
    so?
  What have I said to cause you such affright?

AMALIA.

Affright, señor? I never felt serener. . .
  Does Doña Amalia to your suit consent?

LORENZO.

Ah, more's the pity, I've not yet even seen her!
  I came from Cordova with this intent.

AMALIA.

And yet . . you adore her, never having met

LORENZO.

Oft has her picture made these fond eyes glow !
Her father, Don Hilario, in a letter,
    Sent it me ere he died, three years ago.

AMALIA.

Indeed ?   (He speaks the truth, if ever man did !)

LORENZO.

Our sires long since, while we were children, sw
That we should wed. . .   But later, to be candi
    I turned my nose up at the whole affair.

AMALIA.

Quite sensible !

LORENZO.

            My father, growing furious,
Packed me to Italy and bade me stay.
There, in a mood half scornful and half curious,
    I drew Amalia's picture forth, one day .   .   .

AMALIA.

And closelier studied it ?

LORENZO.

I did. . . Ah, presto !
The scales from off my vision fell at once.
I issued to myself a manifesto,
  Calling myself an idiot, dolt and dunce !

AMALIA.

I had believed you gentlemen were never
  Half such unbiassed critics of yourselves.

LORENZO.

It seemed as if I'd been bewitched by clever
  Contrivances of unpropitious elves !
But now the enchantment vanished. . . As I
  entered
  Into rapt contemplation of her face,
The ideal of all rare womanhood was centered
  There in that portrait's priceless little space !

AMALIA.

You found her so adorable a creature ?

LORENZO.

I found her, save mere wings, an angel quite !

AMALIA.

Perhaps her wings were, after all a feature
  The artist had omitted.

LORENZO (*suddenly agitated*).

                    Does my sight
Play tricks with me ?

AMALIA.'

    What means your agitation ?

LORENZO (*with long sigh*).

Ah, no !   I thought her picture was like you.   .   .
But now I realize the hallucination.   .   .

AMALIA.

You realize it ?   I am glad you do !

LORENZO.

Oh, yes.   'Tis   chance   resemblance   .   .   nothing
    nearer,
As this, my closer gaze at you avers.
Less feminine, sedater and austerer,
    Your face, I'm sure, could never smile like hers !

AMALIA.

And yet I've heard Amalia is reputed
    To be a damsel cold beyond her kind.

LORENZO.

Oh, that's because no man has ever suited
    The moods of her superior soul and mind.

AMALIA.

You are then confident that you can win her?

LORENZO.

Yes, perfectly.

AMALIA.

How dexterous you must be!

LORENZO.

I hope to prove so . . Well, as I'm a sinner,
You're wonderfully like her!—yet not she!

AMALIA.

Where lies our difference! Is it large or slender!

LORENZO.

Her tongue, like yours, could play no waspish part!
She'd not revile, like you, the whole male gender;
Amalia has a woman's loving heart!

AMALIA.

Are you so sure?

LORENZO.

Beyond all chance of error!
No fate would she more eagerly eschew—
None would she hold in more disgust and terror—
Than for an instant to be thought a shrew!

AMALIA.

A shrew ?   Then I'm one ?

LORENZO.

By your own confession . . .

Ah ! Heaven ! (*Seems ill.*)

AMALIA.

You shudder ; you're in pain, I know !

LORENZO.

Forgive my fleeting loss of self-possession ;
That wretched fall of mine upset me so !

AMALIA.

The sherbet—let me not postpone it longer ;
This drop of cordial—let me pour it in.
There . .   your restorative will now be stronger ;
The sherbet by itself was far too thin.

LORENZO (*drinking*).

Thanks—many thanks !

AMALIA (*now very amiable*).

'Twill aid, though scarcely cure you ;
Bruises like yours are not such light mishaps '

LORENZO.

Oh, I'm not bruised.   It's only, I assure you,
A kind of neurological collapse,

AMALIA.

I see—exhaustion, faintness, general sinking . .

LORENZO.

Just that! How well you comprehend my case! . .
But you seem puzzled . .

AMALIA.

I was merely thinking
You've not one sign of illness in your face.

LORENZO.

Ah, but my feelings!

AMALIA (*very sweetly*).

Are they still so painful?
I'll call a doctor, then, without delay. . .

LORENZO.

Please don't! A doctor would be simply baneful;
You're all the doctor I desire to-day.

AMALIA.

But I of medicine have no real knowledge.

LORENZO.

You've more, depend on it, than you suppose;
I'd stake its worth against a whole wise college
Of big-wigs, each with spectacles on nose.

AMALIA (*spreading her fan*).

Instruct me, then ; I'll do whate'er I'm able. .
It might perhaps relieve you to be fanned ?

LORENZO (*weakly*).

No. . . but it would be strangely comfortable
If you'd consent to have me hold your hand.

AMALIA.

My hand ! (*She gives it reluctantly.*)

LORENZO.

There . . that way . . Oh, how unexpected !
My sense of soft repose is actual bliss ;
Often, when we are nervously affected,
We need a soothing tonic, such as this !

AMALIA.

(His hand's quite feverish !)

LORENZO.

You were merely fooling ;
You *don't* hate men as fiercely as you said ?

AMALIA.

Oh, yes ; experience is a rigid schooling ;
Three dear girl-friends of mine have all been wed.

LORENZO.

And all unhappily?

AMALIA.

Yes, all! . . Though zealous
With peace and love their home-lives to anoint,
If they but wink their lords are madly jealous.

LORENZO.

Whom do they wink *at*? There's the dubious
point.

AMALIA.

Poor Isabel! poor Clara! poor Dolores!
You three have shown me matrimony's hurts!

LORENZO.

Have they, indeed? *O tempora! O mores!*
I'll wager they're all three inveterate flirts!

AMALIA.

And why?

LORENZO.

Because the wife who's always babbling
Of how her husband teems with jealous doubt,
Has usually known he does through dabbling
In such queer deeds herself she's been found out!

AMALIA.

Then do you mean that there are husbands tender,
Considerate, kind, unselfish?

LORENZO (*half rising from couch*).

Thousands! Yes!
Husbands whose joy and pride it is to render
Their wives more loyalty than words express!

AMALIA.

And dearly love them, too?

LORENZO.

With adoration!

AMALIA.

Oh, what beatitude your answer paints!

LORENZO (*springing up*).

How's this? You smile! That smile is confirmation!
Amalia! You are she, by all the Saints!

AMALIA.

Grant it. But wherefore stand you thus, inspecting
My face with looks that pierce me like a blade?

LORENZO.

Oh, 'tis because I cannot help reflecting
How scandalously I've been duped—betrayed!

AMALIA.

You stare like one whom reason hath forsaken.

LORENZO.

'*Tis* my Amalia !   No, I am *not* distraught !
Here, before consciousness could well awaken—
   Here—here—to your abode have I been brought !

AMALIA.

And if you have !   What then ?

LORENZO.

                  What then ?   Delusion
   Unmerciful as ever man befell !

AMALIA.

Nay, hear me, Don Lorenzo, I——

LORENZO.

                        Confusion !
   Thus to be tricked !   I'll go at once.   Farewell.

AMALIA.

Why are you angered?

LORENZO.

                  Why?   And can you ask it?
   Have I not let you gaze on my heart's core ?—
As one that shows within some sacred casket
   Gems he has hid there and has gloated o'er !

AMALIA.

But stay ! This love you speak of with contrition—
Was it not meant for me alone to prize?

LORENZO.

Yes—but on terms of honored recognition,
Not when I met you mantled in disguise !

AMALIA.

Disguise I sought not.

LORENZO.

You that hate all men so,
An icicle, indeed !—farewell once more !

AMALIA.

You must not go yet . . you're too ill .
Lorenzo !

LORENZO.

True ; I am ill . .

AMALIA.

Remain, then, I implore !

LORENZO.

And if I *should* remain ! What hope of guerdon
Exists for one that loves thee as do I ?
Thou'rt far too proud a maid beneath love's burden
Ever to stoop thyself ! . .

AMALIA (*meekly*).

But I might try.

LORENZO.

"Might try!"   Is Paradise its gates unclosing?

AMALIA.

I *will* try!

LORENZO.

Oh, Amalia, this to *me* ?

AMALIA.

Thee only!

(*They embrace, as* ANITA *enters, peering about.*)

ANITA.

How's our patient?   Still reposing?
Or has he awakened? . .   Powers of mercy! see!

LORENZO.

Well, good Anita?

ANITA.

So . .   your arm is belting
Her waist!   Ah, sight more welcome I ne'er saw!

LORENZO.

It means your icicle at last is melting.

AMALIA (*weeping*).

Oh, yes !   These tell-tale drops announce its thaw.

ANITA.

Dear lady !   And may no future frost re-weld it !

LORENZO.

Trust *me* . .   my sunshine will be far too warm !

AMALIA (*merrily*).

What icicle, when sunshine hath dispelled it,
Can ever freeze again to its old form ?

COURAGE !

Be brave, O man, and face your fate,
For death is your divorceless mate,
And all the creeds that claim to save
Your soul beyond the hungry grave
Are sieves that stoop their leaking sides
In thankless though mysterious tides.
The God they name as mercy's might
May live in music, flowers and light,
But if at all his kingship be,
Night, pest, fire, earthquake still are he.
The path you tread, from birth to bier,
Through meadowy calms may slope and veer,
Blessed amply, for a fleeting while,
By destiny's effulgent smile,
Yet rest you sure that ere it cease
Dread storm will trench upon its peace.
For ages of desire and prayer ;
Ages when faith defied despair ;
Ages of bigotry so crude
Swine were its fit similitude ;

Ages that history's worst gloom dims,
When Christ and crime were synonyms ;
Ages when freedom's huge form waked,
While churches rocked, while priestcraft quaked,
While Valkyr reason caught the brand
Of justice in its virgin hand—
Nay, all that variant search has taught
Alike by suffering and by thought—
All tells one tale, through records vast :
Life means mere mockery, first and last.

And yet be brave to face your fate,
O man, howe'er with massive weight
Far worse than captive brutes may know,
The doom of living crush you low.
Think, though your bondage seem austere,
What brother bondsmen you may cheer,
And how the balm of love's glad breath
May almost pluck the sting from death.
Mark, too, that though their term endures
But briefly, glorious joys are yours—
The joys of lovers, parents, kin ;
Of arts wide heaven to wander in ;
Of friendships rare ; of potions pure

At lofty fonts of literature ;
Nor less than these, of Nature's far
And bounteous boons, from leaf to star ;—
Yet still those joys' more splendid span
Of mercy and help to fellow-man !

So, nerved by stoic patience, dare
The glacial glances of despair ;
And though life turn you worn and wan,
Die bravely, with your harness on !

Ah, courage, courage, faltering souls !
Perchance to paradisiac goals
The race moves ; and if this be true,
Each individual deed ye do
Fraternity's diviner way,
Will speed that large millennial day
When men shall walk, bright-browed and grand,
Our beauteous planet's wrong-cursed land !